Fishing
with
the
Devil

and

other fiendish tales

Sheldon

Enjoy!

Coffin Hop Press

Fishing with the Devil

and

other fiendish tales

Robert Bose

Illustrated by
James Beveridge

COFFIN HOP PRESS LTD.
CANADA

Fishing with the Devil and other fiendish tales

Robert Bose – First Edition

Copyright © 2017 Coffin Hop Press Ltd.

Coffin Hop Press Ltd.
200 Rivervalley Crescent SE
Calgary, Alberta Canada T2C 3K8
www.coffinhop.com

Publisher's Note: This is a work of fiction. Names, characters, places, and incidents are a product of the author's imagination. Locales and public names are sometimes used for atmospheric purposes. Any resemblance to actual people, living or dead, or to businesses, companies, events, institutions, or locales is completely coincidental.

Book design © 2017 BookDesignTemplates.com

Illustrations by James Beveridge

Fishing with the Devil ©2015 originally published in *In Places Between*, August 2015

A Dead Reckoning ©2015 originally published in *AB Negative* Coffin Hop Press Ltd.

Fallen ©2016 originally published in *In Places Between*, August 2016

Gambling with Ghosts © 2016 originally published as *Hot Blooded* in *Enigma Front: Burnt* Analemma Books

ISBN 978-0-9947378-2-3

For my beautiful wife,
who ignores most of the insanity.

Contents

FOREWORD

What can I tell you about Robert Bose? He's a little fella. We both are.

It works out well when we happen to sit together at events. It's easy for other people to see over our heads. We can sit in the front row - unobtrusively. We tend to see eye-to-eye: proverbially, metaphorically, and quite literally.

Rob may be of less-than-intimidating stature, but he keeps a tiny sledgehammer in his pocket. Let me tell you, man, that hammer packs a Thor-sized wallop. When it's loaded for bear and aimed squarely at the page, Rob wields his literary weapon exactly like a Viking God, raining down thunder and lightning and pure artistic badassery. Whether it's a sci-fi tale of Empirical corruption and greed; a hardboiled mashup of Chinese Alchemean sorcery and two-fisted tough guys; A mysterious, grime-filled hole-in-the-wall; Murder on a movie set; the magical properties of a ball-bearing in the winner-takes-all game of high-stakes marbles; or the semi-autobiographical title story *Fishing with the Devil*, Rob infuses everything he writes with a tidal undercurrent of mysticism, and a great, unknowable weirdness, just beyond the periphery of our faulty human vision. Nothing is ever so simple as black and white. Everything you perceive as reality is just flickering images, playing against a gently fluttering curtain that just barely covers the doorway to another dimension, another *universe,* where anything and everything is possible.

Can you hear it? The thunder? The rumbling vibrations of the coming storm, climbing up through your bones and rattling your teeth? That curtain is about to tear wide and ignite in a firestorm of magic and mayhem. So, give that tiny sledgehammer a wide berth, and prepare to be rocked into oblivion.

Rob Bose is here, and his legends are colossal.

Axel Howerton
Editor, pal, raconteur
Calgary, AB, Canada
June 2017

1

First Round's on Me

His back to a wall, the Devil stared Death in the face.

"I'm glad you could make it," he said. "It's been ages."

Death, an older, hard-eyed woman in black motorcycle leathers, brushed a few strands of hair behind an ear, rested a boot on an extra chair, and leaned against her knee. "Would it kill you to ask me to dinner without an ulterior motive?"

"It's not like that."

"Oh, please. How long have we known each other?"

"Forever."

"Then don't be a bore."

A waitress wandered up. "Would you like something from the bar? A cocktail perhaps?"

"Oh, yes," said Death. "What would you recommend, Lucy?"

His eye twitched. "Ever had a Bloody Caesar?"

"No, but it sounds exquisite. I'll try one."

"Excellent," said the waitress. She turned to the Devil. "And yourself?"

"Lagavulin, the older the better."

"Very good. I'll give you a few minutes to look over the menu. Today's special is flame grilled lamb sirloin with braised shelling beans and mint gremolata."

They studied the menu until their drinks arrived. The Devil raised his tumbler. "Cin cin."

"Cheers," said Death, studying the stick of celery jutting from her glass.

The Devil took a sip, half-closed his eyes, and let out a contented sigh. "How's the immortal soul storage business?"

"Never been busier. Hell?"

"Never been hotter."

She laughed. "Wow, didn't see that coming. More small talk or do you want to get down to business?"

"Well," he looked past her, through the window of the restaurant, watching the street lamps flicker to life. "I'm in a rough spot. I could use some help."

"Of course you do." Death leaned back, wiggled around to get comfortable. "You know the deal. Tell me some lies. Good ones. None of those dreadful fishing stories you love so much. Make me laugh. Make me care."

The Devil shot back his whiskey and cleared his throat. "Funny you should mention fishing."

2

Fishing with the Devil

The Devil came for me early. He knocked once, little more than a tap, before strolling in and announcing breakfast with his usual booming gusto. "Bacon and beer Lil, the breakfast of choice for young ladies and chthonic champions."

My stomach gurgled and I feigned death, head under a pillow, until he laughed and walked away. After a short and unsuccessful attempt to steal more winks, I yawned, pulled on a long flannel shirt and stumbled down the stairs of the old country lodge, following the wafting scent of bacon. The Devil put down his morning news, stood up, and greeted me with a warm hug.

"Good to see you survived the night," he said, picking a speck of lint from his black silk pajamas, over which flopped an apron proclaiming 'If you can't stand the fire, stay out of my kitchen.' On the obsidian countertop, an enameled tin plate held a stack of pancakes slathered in maple syrup and butter. Thank heavens; I might survive this after all.

The Devil dropped three massive slabs of bacon on the edge of the plate and winked. "Extra crispy," he said, pulling up a stool and taking a long draft from an ornate black stein.

I dove in, hungrier than I thought. "Aren't you going to have some *Nonno*?"

"No, lass, I have this to keep my strength up." Her grandfather took another pull.

"Could I get a drink? Orange juice or maybe chocolate milk?" A girl could hope.

He collected a silver mug from the cupboard, filled it from a pony keg on the counter, and slid it under my nose. "Bacon *and* beer, as promised."

The smell of brimstone made my eyes water.

"An Infernal Stout, it'll put hair on your chest and meat on your bones. You're thin as a rail. What do they feed you up there?"

I didn't need any hair on my chest, and mother would freak when she found out, but after I got past the screaming soul in the foam head, I managed a tentative sip. Not bad. It filled me with warmth and made my face tingle. "Uh, thanks."

"It's the least I can do. Just don't tell your mother." He let me finish the meal and started washing up. "Now, to the question of the day, where shall we fish?"

Oh right, the fishing... "What are our choices?"

The Devil dug up a map and spread it across the island. "Let's see, there's Lost Lake, Purgatory Pools, Revenant Reservoir, and the Sea of the Damned. How ambitious are you feeling?"

I tapped a dark body of water in the farthest corner. It was hidden under his stein but the blood red glyphs surrounding it drew my attention. "What about this one?"

He tugged on his ear and moved his mug out of the way. "That's the Abyss, a terrible hole. One of the few places down here not under my control. Old Momma Levi and I haven't been on the best of terms since that time I went fishing with Job."

My heart skipped a beat at the thought of danger. I was fourteen and my mother still stressed about me crossing the street without supervision. The old man watched my face out of the corner of his eye and nodded. "Well, if you insist. The Abyss it is."

"I'm not insisting!"

"Nonsense. No promises that we'll catch anything, but I can guarantee adventure." Without further discussion, he went off to prepare.

I wandered upstairs and dug out my phone. No service. Not that I had expected any, but I was starting to get twitchy. I flopped on the bed and stared at the ceiling. Fishing, really? It wasn't what I should be doing this weekend. I'd planned to head to the mall with my friends, do a bit of shopping, and sample a new Ben and Jerry's flavour, *Oat of this Swirled*. Fishing with the Devil hadn't even been on the radar. Sure, he'd always threatened, on his rare visits, to bring me down here, show me the sights, but mom always found an excuse to keep it from happening. They'd never seen eye to eye on anything, especially me. I found my flip-flops and went outside to wait on the front steps.

A smoky haze clung to the surrounding countryside like a comfortable blanket. Warm, cozy, and almost pleasant. Not the 'I want to leave my life and stay here' kind of pleasant, but scenic in an old post card sort of way. One faded picture flashed across my mind: my parents, backpacking in Yosemite on their honeymoon, Half Dome rising majestically in the background. When they were young, when they were in love.

I heard the car before I saw it, a rumbling black monster sheathed in chrome, dragging a silver cabin cruiser sporting stylized flames and enormous jet engines. "Nice boat, *Nonno*." I rolled my eyes. I guess you didn't need to be subtle when you were Lord of the Underworld.

The Devil stuck his head out the window. "Hop in." I went to open the back door but he stopped me with a bark. "No, up front." The enormous seat swallowed me up, the supple leather pure first-class luxury. I reached for the seatbelt that wasn't there. "Do you really think you'd need it?" he laughed as he gunned the engine and sped out onto the road, spraying a mass of chewed up pumice into the air behind us.

I held on for dear life, or death, and we rocketed out onto the blacktop. The Devil produced a massive cigar, bit off the end, and spit the tip out the window. "Be a darling and light me up."

I fumbled around looking for a lighter. He mumbled something like 'Haven't you learned anything yet' and grabbed my hand. "Think about fire." I gave him a vacant stare. He sighed. "Think about making your thumb burst into flame. Concentrate."

Nothing happened.

"Come on now, it's not hard."

Still nothing.

"Dammit child. Close your eyes. Imagine your thumb is hot. Imagine it starting to smolder. Imagine it starting to burn. If it doesn't, yell at it, force it to."

I did as he said, mentally screaming at my thumb, and after a few seconds a small flame appeared. He leaned over and lit the cigar. "That's a neat trick," I said, astonished, and amused myself by flicking my thumb on and off.

"Keep practicing, it's in your blood." He took a deep draw and pulled out another huge stogie. "Want one?"

I coughed.

"There are smaller ones in a box under the seat." When I turned to stare out the window, he got the hint and changed the subject. "So, how's Lilith?"

"You know mom. Bound and determined to dominate everyone and everything at the office."

"I imagine she won't stop till she's burnt the firm to the ground. Those old gnomes are tangling with the wrong hellcat."

"Yeah. I wouldn't even be here, but she had some critical board meeting in Zurich this weekend and you ended up being her last choice. She was frantic."

He nodded. "No doubt. And how are you enjoying Witchwood Academy? I'd say your sorcery training needs work if you haven't even mastered minor flame calling yet."

"Sorcery training? I go to Devonshire Middle School. Grade eight."

"So, no sorcery at all..."

"Mom says I'm spiritually conflicted, that I have no aptitude for that sort of thing."

"What? That's..." He shook his head and frowned. "That's bullshit, pardon my language. What the hell is your mother thinking? Regular school. Are you studying *anything* useful there?"

"Violin."

"Hmm, the fiddle, that's encouraging, for a second there I thought you were going to say recorder," he shuddered, "or ukulele."

We debated the merits of various tunes for an hour until the caddy rolled up to a long-neglected dock, rotting wood covered in spiked barnacles. An endless expanse of dark water stretched away, flat and placid but leaking an aura of old evil and menace, the air thick with death and decay. The Abyss. Lovely place.

The Devil backed the boat into the water and we blasted out into the unknown. Grandfather scanned the horizon and took a drink from a small flask.

"I'm guessing you've never fished before? "

"No, but I've seen people do it on TV."

He groaned. "How old are you? Have you learned *anything* useful?"

I shrugged, annoyed but not rising to his bait, and examined the rod, an elaborate rig sprouting from the back of the boat, complete with a comfortable seat and umbrella. The translucent silver line shimmered in the light of the distant sky fires.

"Adamant, proof against anything in Heaven or Hell," he commented, "your Uncle Baal made the line, hook, rod, and boat for me as a favour. Flexible, light, and unbreakable, but the stuff is damn near impossible to work with. I think he's still cursing about it."

The Devil dropped a bucket down next to the chair and flipped off the lid. "Thread one of these little buggers onto the end and don't let it bite you." A motley collection of severed Imp heads, all bulging crimson eyes and serrated teeth, glared up at me. I managed to avoid being nipped, jammed the hook into one without thinking because uh ugh, and played out the line.

"Do I even what to know what we are fishing for?"

"Bone-backs or maybe Abyssal Sculpin if we get lucky."

Delightful. I settled in and tried to get comfortable. It was terribly boring and the low growl of the engine soon threatened to lull me to sleep. I yawned and stretched.

"So, is Gabriel, your father, still..." he paused, staring into the murky water.

"Dead? Missing? Off on some inter-dimensional mission for God? He's a deadbeat if that's what you were asking."

"Damn archangels, they are all the same. I don't know what your mother ever saw in him."

"She says he was handsome and charming. Swept her off her feet."

"I always thought I'd raised her better than that."

My rod bent and the line went taunt. I held on tight as a powerful force took the bait and went deep. "Got one."

"Nice, just give it some slack, take your time, and let it tire itself out. No need to hurry."

Following his directions, I relaxed and pretended I knew what I was doing. "Mom still loves him, if that's what you're asking, still has his picture on her nightstand. I've seen her holding it to her chest when she thinks I'm not watching. I wish he hadn't left."

The Devil didn't say anything.

After what felt like forever and a day our fish surfaced and we got a look at what I'd hooked. It was an immense, armour plated grey crocodile sprouting hundreds of writhing puckered tentacles. Narrow, glowing eyes turned to glare at us, righteously pissed off. "Yuck! What is that thing?"

"Heaven's breath lass, that's a baby leviathan. We'd better let it go and get out of here before its mother shows up. Like I said at breakfast, I'm not in her good books these days."

The sea began to boil for half a mile around.

"Or not, damn it."

"So?" I let go of the rod, impending doom washing over me.

The Devil thought for a moment. "The rod is part of the boat. We'll have to sever the line."

"I thought you said it was unbreakable, that nothing in Heaven or Hell could damage it."

"It is, but you can cut it."

"Me?"

"You have both demonic and angelic blood, of Heaven and Hell, yet bound by neither. Just use your powers."

"I don't have any powers. I told you what mom said."

The sea was a frothy mess. The Devil had the jets at full but the monster began pulling us further from the distant shore. "Stop saying that, of course you do. Summon something sharp before she has us for lunch."

"How?"

"Just like you did with the flame in the car. Concentrate. Think about fire and light."

I had no clue what to do. Massive tentacles rose from the depths around us, overpowering me with the smell of death, like the rotting, maggoty jackrabbit we'd found on the lawn one year, but infinitely worse.

"Can't you get us out of here? Magic us away or something?"

"No. I might be able to save myself, if I have to, but now that she's realized what you are, and I know she has, she will never let you go. Never in a million years."

"But you're the DEVIL. You can do anything!"

"That's not how it works here."

ROBERT BOSE

Tentacles found the boat and started tearing off the parts that weren't indestructible. I dodged a flailing limb that smashed our picnic basket. I didn't have any powers. The flame in the car was just a cheap trick. Wasn't it?

A cloak of shadow and fire started to coalesce around grandfather. The tentacles smouldered and melted away when they touched him, but more kept appearing. He stood up. Loomed.

"Lil. Child. Stop messing around, I mean it. This is real. If you don't cut the line, you are going to die, or worse. She'll take your soul and turn you into a monster. Is that what you want?"

"Of course not."

"Then use your god damned powers!"

"But, I just don't—"

He cut me off. "Excuses. All I hear are excuses. I can see why your father left, you really are useless. Goodbye Lil." He transformed into a dancing flame and shot skyward, leaving me to my fate.

I staggered, abandoned. Useless? He was useless. Just like my father. Leaving me alone, leaving me when I needed him the most. My anger burned hot. Bright. And, just like that, a sword appeared in my hand, a blade of golden flame. A bright aura surrounded me, infusing me, turning wrath into purpose.

The Adamant line resisted. I braced myself and sawed through it while pausing to slice apart some pesky tentacles intent on pulling me overboard. The severed bits, still squirming and searching, dissipated under my aura, leaving behind nothing more than a greasy mist. Without warning the line broke with a thunderclap, tossing me to the deck as the boat rocketed away, the engines still set to full.

Reappearing with a gentle pop, the Devil got the cruiser under control, avoiding my rage filled glare. I looked back to see an island sized creature emerge from the depths, felt her mind brush mine, felt her power, felt her promise. We didn't slow down.

With a screeching, sideways drift, the Devil slid up to the portal and let me out. I grabbed my bags from the trunk and went over to his window, still not sure how I felt about him. I understood why he'd done it, but that didn't make it right, didn't make it acceptable. But then again, he was the Devil. I guess I'd forgotten that.

He didn't say anything for a few seconds, eventually giving me a nod of grudging approval. "You're going to have to make a choice soon Lilim, a tough choice. A war is coming and while you are of both Heaven and Hell, neither binds you. Don't forget that."

I held his eyes for a moment. Ancient and endless, mirrors of darkness and fire, twins of that great beast from the Abyss. "I won't."

I stepped across the line, hand in my pocket, flicking my thumb on and off.

3

A Hole

I regarded the hole, a patch of darkness marring the bathroom ceiling, from the comfort of Amy's bathtub. A trick of the light? A convergence of shadow thrown by dusty spider webs draping every nook and cranny? I couldn't tell. Besides, with my head jackhammering behind the polka dotted pink shower curtains, everything looked, and felt, full of holes.

Fragments of broken memory forced their way free of my subconscious, fluttering like a bat with a broken wing. Last night, a rough one, filled with drinking, dancing, and debauchery at the bar down the street. I'd kissed the girl from upstairs. Tina. More than kissed, god help me, I'd shagged her, shagged her silly. And what the hell had they been sliding down the bar? Tequila shooters?

Prairie Fires? I'd drunk them all, under protest of course, until they burned through my gut, liquefying every organ in a hellfire infused apocalypse. I'd realized, somehow, that the end was near, and dragged myself out of Tina's embrace, sprinted home, and delivered a double-ended salute with chest to thighs, arms wrapped around cold porcelain.

The hole. Right. A burst pipe? The crumbling old tenement, a low-end seventies era rental complete with cracked brown tile and faux wood paneling, bore the scars of decades. I never understand why Amy, my girlfriend and sugar mommy, stayed. Dirt-cheap, sure, but she could do better. Not that it mattered. Once the little lady got wind of my escapades at the Fang and Gill, and she would, I doubt I'd ever see the place again, or any place again, for that matter.

With a shudder, my brain skipped a beat and tossed me into a labyrinth of guilt-ridden dreams where temptation lurked behind every corner.

❖❖❖

I teetered on the lip of Hell and looked down. Way down. Devil girls shouted and urged, squealed and pointed to an inviting bed, a jumble of rich purple pillows. Jumped? No, never. Pushed.

I fell, landing dead center, and bounced once. The bed engulfed me, pulling me in, pulling me deep. Something sharp pushed against my back, penetrating, pushing through. Bloody points protruded from my chest like twisted dead fingernails.

❖❖❖

My eyes snapped open, the echo of my shriek sliding away behind a blanket of laboured breathing. "Who's there?" leaked from my parched throat before I realized the death rattle was mine.

Sitting up induced a round of dry heaves and a trickle of florescent green bile that dribbled down my chin and puke encrusted shirt. Grim, even for me. I pulled myself up to the sink, peeled off shirt and pants, and dug through the bathroom vanity for something, anything to take the edge off. No luck. I found makeup, feminine hygiene products, toothbrushes, shavers, and a large unmarked bottle of white powder. Cocaine? Rat poison? Not worth the risk, not even close. I tossed the bottle back in the drawer and took a drink from the minty fresh toothbrush cup, spit out the congealed blobs, and contemplated striking out towards the kitchen and beyond, the greener pastures of the bedroom calling.

The hole called louder.

Not a leak. No water and no staining, just an irregular slash, eight inches across, and black as night. I stepped up on the toilet seat to get a better look and slipped on some vomit.

"Bloody fucking hell," I screamed, flailing and falling to smash the side of my head on the claw footed bathtub. Blood joined the puke and other bodily fluids. Dead? Not quite. If anything, the pain and shock pushed me up the sober scale a notch. Lucky break I hadn't hurt anything important.

Another groaning trip to the sink, another splash of water, and another grotesque reflection hardened my resolve. I tossed a soiled towel over the toilet, grabbed a plunger, and stepped onto the seat, fighting a round of vertigo and chest rending dry heaves. Upwards and onwards, the wooden handle met resistance after a foot and a half, a firmness that gave when I pushed harder. I pulled the plunger out with a squelch and watched something earthy, viscous, and hairy drip from the end of it, an old, putrid smell permeating the air. The water gurgling in my innards didn't stay down.

Delightful, a decomposing rat, exactly what Amy needed in modern bathroom ceiling insulation. A second poke, for good measure, invoked the faint sound of claws on wood. Correction, a decaying rat still clinging to some semblance of life. The landlord, the bug eyed peeping tom Mr. Marina, had warned Amy and I about the local vermin, describing their lack of virtue with a toothy sneer and air quote claws. I thought he'd been talking about the punk living next door, or the ultra-creeps across the way, but I guess he'd been literal for a change. Vigorous prodding failed to dislodge the critter and provoked a muffled squeal from its expiring lungs.

Why me? Why now? Sinister holes and dying rats, hallucinations and hang overs – I didn't deserve this grief. Doomed, that's what I was, but maybe, just maybe, if I sorted out this rat problem, Amy would forgive me. I climbed to the top of the toilet tank, steadied myself against the wall, and jammed in my arm.

Warm. Gooey. The rat, a huge sucker, shifted when I got my hand on it, and with the touch, a moment of clarity. An ear. Not a tiny, furry, rat ear, a god damned human ear attached to a god damned human head of short, moist hair.

Why did these things happen to me? One moment of weakness, one tiny lapse in judgment, and my life goes from aspiring slacker alcoholic to the next sacrificial victim on a straight-to-video episode of *Ghouls Gone Wild*.

I snatched back my arm, planning on making a break for the relative safety of any other place on the planet, when a hand clamped down on my wrist and yanked hard, jerking me into the hole.

"Shit! Shit! Shit!" I yelled, my head bouncing off the ceiling a number of times before the jerker realized I wouldn't fit and stopped the yoyo. I ended up wedged tight, right up to my shoulder, and belted out one final spirited "Shiiiiit!" for good measure. Pinned, toes dangling inches above the toilet top, I flailed, kicking the walls and punching the ceiling. It didn't help.

The iron grip tightened, grinding my wrist bones, and lightning lanced through my shoulder and out of my eyes, forcing tears and a sob as I yet again reflected on my impending doom. Had I brought this upon myself? Was *I* the villain in this sordid tale? I croaked out a feeble laugh. Hell no. Women, temptation, I was under a spell, as usual.

Adrenaline burned away the remaining legacy of last night's brain fog and my thoughts churned. Tina's flat sat directly above. The hole went up. Therefore, the hole connected to Tina's flat. Was she some sort of monstrous serial killer? She hadn't felt inhumanly strong, had soft, well moisturized skin, and those lips... No, it couldn't be her.

Time to make sure, however. "Tina! TINA! TIIIINNNNAAA!" No response.

I screamed for the trailer trash punk that lived next door. He listened to hair metal bands night and day, blasting his *music* on oversized headphones, but maybe, just maybe, he'd head out for a smoke. Nothing. I almost screamed for the pale androgynous, almost certainly incestuous twins across the way, but thought better of it. I'd rather die than have them find me like this. Amy? Amy worked irregular hours. She might be home in hours or days.

My father always told me "God helps those who help themselves". He loved that proverb. Me, not so much, it sounded like work, but I didn't have a choice. I grunted, groaned, and shoved with my free hand. Not a budge. I walked up the wall and planted both feet where ceiling met wall, engaging my quads and gaining leverage. Better. The harder I pushed, however, the tighter the grip became, an ever-increasing vice. My wrist grated and I couldn't feel my fingers. Blood trickled down my chest, escaping the rough edge of the hole where my shoulder hadn't plugged it.

When I ran out of energy I flopped, defeated, to hang twitching. I heard my phone's ringtone echo from time to time until the batteries died. I watched the slow drip from the grimy sink faucet for a while. It offset the irregular trickle of blood into my eye when I looked up. Sleep, or unconsciousness, crowded in.

❖❖❖

Drifting pot smoke providing a warm buzz and throbbing dance music pounding my frame, I went looking for a drink. The bartender flashed his fangs and shouted over the clamour. "What can I get for you?"

"A Red Bull vodka."

He twisted his lip in a sneer. "Figures, and for your mauve friend?"

"Who?"

Twisted dead fingernails traced a bloody line down my arm. "Forget about me already darling?"

❖❖❖

I came back to life, the ethereal dream voice ringing in my head. Damn, where the hell had that come from? Before the answer presented itself, the nagging urge to piss overwhelmed me. Arm numb, I fumbled with my boxers, shredded during last night's adventure, a victim of Tina's under-the-table ministrations. The ventilated cloth tore further, the elastic down to a thread. I fire hosed the sink, impressed with my aim, and managed to snap the remaining thread with a brisk shake. My boxers, or what remained of them, slipped to dangle from a toe.

"What in the blazing seventy-seventh level of hell is going on here?" A short, stocky redhead in black leather bondage gear stood in the bathroom doorway. Amy.

"Thank god." I rasped.

She wrinkled her nose and stepped close, careful to avoid my worst excesses. "Is this some kind of autoerotic asphyxiation thing? I'm not judging, but if that's your gig, you really need to put down plastic first."

I grimaced. "Ha, ha, no. I was trying to pull a dead rat out of this hole but found a... a body instead. Now someone upstairs, someone insanely strong, is trying to add me to their collection."

Amy glanced at the ceiling, shrugged, and snagged my boxers where they hung. She examined a bright smear. "Explain."

"What? I've had a rough morning."

She pressed my underwear into a tight ball and flipped them into the garbage bin. "Lipstick,

Purple Pomegranate. I only wear Red Death."
Crimson lips curled.

I deflated. "It's not my fault. I swear to god."

"Of course, it isn't." Amy gave the ceiling a suspicious look, scratched her freckled nose, and narrowed her eyes. She knew who lived in the flat above. "Wait here, I'll go up and check it out." She came back a moment later, took a selfie with me in the background, and left chuckling.

I closed my eyes.

❖❖❖

The rat waddled across the hardwood floor, weaving and teetering like a tiny Jack Sparrow, tripping over its own feet and colliding with chair legs. It reached a plate of nachos abandoned near a glowing purple hole in the wall and stopped, dropping a load of steaming pellets and salivating over the crusty chips and mouldy cheese. A hand emerged from the hole, twisted dead fingernails reaching out to snag the rat's tail, dragging the scrambling rodent into the maw as it scarfed down the appetizer in a flurry of frantic bites.

❖❖❖

Distant shouting blasted me awake, the smell of sex and cheddar thick in the air. A blood-curdling scream. An earth-shattering thump. The room shook and I crashed down, bouncing off the toilet to land where I'd started, skirting consciousness in a pool of bodily fluids. The hole folded in on itself and vanished.

"Rise and shine asshole." Amy prodded my head with a steel-toed boot and rested a gore dripping fire axe against the bathroom doorframe. "Looks like you need a Band-Aid."

My arm tingled, heavy and unresponsive. No pain, at least in comparison to my head, my back, and every bloody bone in my body. I heaved the arm up on the third try and shrieked. My hand, or rather, my skeletal claw, the bloody points ending in twisted dead fingernails, glistened in the harsh fluorescent light. Teeth marks scored the bones, ligaments, and tendons.

Amy sat down on the toilet seat and lit a cigarette, blew smoke in my screaming face. "You were right about one thing lover boy, that was some rat."

4

Running the Red

Sigrid ran across the rusty boulder field, suspended dust obscuring cosmic impacts and volcanic formations. On a different day, she'd have savoured the experience. Today, it was just another obstacle. She slipped into her zone and picked up speed, letting the Martian surface flow by, letting her mind wander. It didn't wander far. The face danced in the thin atmosphere. The face that haunted her thoughts and dreams, the face she glimpsed in every swirl of dust, in every outcropping of rock. It glared, eyes narrow and accusatory, before slamming into her and dispersing with a soundless scream.

A cough tickled her throat. Sips of water pulled from the nipple in her helmet helped, but the cough had other plans. It came hard, dragging the contents of her stomach along with it.

"It glared, eyes narrow and accusatory, before slamming into her and dispersing with a soundless scream."

With a lurching stop, she popped her visor and leaned forward, her protective bio-gel membrane stretching out like a teardrop before breaking away and leaving a soupy sphere freezing on the rocky soil.

Her communicator hummed to life. "Sig, you just lost one hundred and seventy-eight milliliters of fluid and your rebreather is down to twenty-two percent. What's your status?"

"I'm okay Phoebe, just hacked up a lung and more chunks of that damn flu."

The mission controller clicked her tongue. "I knew it was going to come back and haunt you. Didn't I say that, oh about a million times?"

"Did you?" Sig tried to laugh but another cough came out instead.

"Uh-huh. Now slow down and take it easy, you won't be in any condition to save anyone if you drop dead before you reach the top."

"I'm fine, really."

"Stop lying, I have your vitals on screen. Don't make me tap into your camera and play big sister."

"You'd be bored to tears. I'll be okay, I have to be."

"Just make sure you top everything up at the next drop point."

"I will. It's only five kilometers away."

"Seven point two. But who's counting."

"You're not helping, you know that, right?"

"Honesty is the best policy. Now get a move on, you still have thirty-five to make today's target."

"I'm going, I'm going." Sig took a longer drink and got back up to speed, ever bounding across the rock and sand, her eyes scanning for the best path through the treacherous terrain, scanning for faces in the storm, and mind sliding into the zone and the recent past.

THREE DAYS AGO

Following a light knock on Sig's door, Hemi Parata, the little Maori operations chief, poked his head into her workshop, sporting a grin that went on forever.

"Doctor Meyer, the recovery vehicle just limped in through Gate B. Commander Germain is clearing the airlock and will be in the maintenance bay in ten minutes. Phoebe said she'd meet us there."

Sig tried to smile back, without success. "Thanks. I'll head straight down." She'd been listening to the reports as they came in and knew the score, but there was always hope.

Andre Germain, the Tharsis Research Base commander, was climbing out of the dust covered six-wheel exploration crawler when she arrived. He hopped to the floor, handed his helmet to one of the service crew, and shook his head. "The storm is too fierce. Without the solar array charging, the batteries only provided enough power to get to the bottom of the shield ramp. I hoped to push them farther."

"So, nothing?" She already knew the answer. There was no way Devon could have gotten all the way down three hundred plus kilometers of Mons Olympus, in the storm, in two days.

"I couldn't see much and sensors didn't detect anything with all the electrical interference. Devon knows what he's doing. I'm sure he's waiting it out in an emergency shelter."

Hemi punched up the local weather forecast and projected it in front of them. "The storm is big and growing, a rare cyclonic centered directly on the caldera. Might be an active hot pocket causing heat differentials." He squinted at the churning graphics. "It's going to last a month or two."

"Devon doesn't have enough supplies for a month or two." A few days, a week, tops, unless he got down to the next supply station. Sig hugged her arms to her chest. He hadn't though; there'd been no activity or communications from the second highest camp. Something had happened to him. Something bad. She felt it in her heart. "Give me options. There has to be other options."

Phoebe tucked long stray hair behind an ear, flicked the weather projection away. "A shuttle is out of the question. Mars Command made it clear they won't fly into an electrically charged dust storm. Even if they agreed to try, our insurance won't cover it."

"We can't let this come down to money, dammit, he could be dying up there," said Sig. "How far away is Big Ben?" The robotic nuclear transport truck had hauled all the supply canisters up the volcano months ago.

Commander Germain yawned. "Twenty days out. It was already halfway to Hellas Colony." He yawned again and rubbed his eyes. "I'm beat. I need grab a bite and crash."

Phoebe tapped Sig's chest. "When did *you* last sleep? Go take a nap, I'll call Command again and see if they have any other ideas."

Sig nodded and slumped back to her quarters. She paced back and forth, brought up maps of the volcano, running air supply scenarios till she wanted to scream. When she couldn't stand it anymore, she threw herself on a couch and flipped on the news. "—as well as being part of the first team, with his partner and expedition leader Dr. Sigrid Meyer, to dive Ligeia Mare on Titan. Extreme sports icon Devon Atherton has gone missing while attempting to run to the top of Olympus Mons, the highest mountain in the solar system—"

Second highest after Rheasilvia on Vesta, Sig thought to herself, but what the hell did they know. She watched the archival footage of Devon standing on top of Mount Everest, giving the camera a thumbs-up. She'd captured that moment four years ago while they were field-testing prototypes of their slim, body hugging running spacesuits.

"—a solo endeavour after Meyer dropped out due to an undisclosed illness. Reaching the top in a little over seven days, contact with both Atherton, and the summit communication station, was lost when a storm of unexpected severity settled over the mountain."

She hurled her data pad at the wall screen. Devon hadn't wanted to go alone, arguing till the end.

"Sig, we need to do this together. We can postpone the run till you've recovered."

"No, we can't," she said, shivering under a blanket.

"Why?"

"Three reasons. One, the transport has dropped the supplies. We can't leave them out there for months."

"Yes, we can. It's Mars, it's not like someone is going to steal them. And besides, they're weather proof containers, they'll keep."

She ignored him and continued. "Two, our sponsors have a tight timeline for their footage requirements. They'll freak if we delay. You told me that yourself."

"Maybe. I'm sure they'll underst−"

"Three, our bodies are already adapting to the low gravity. We'll lose the advantage of our earth-g strength before long."

"But..."

"No buts." A cough. A sneeze. "You seem to forget who the Expedition Leader is."

In the end he'd given in, a slave to schedules, resources, and the hunger of a billion extreme sport fans. She'd killed him for a bloody TV show.

THE PRESENT

Emblazoned with the Planetary Discovery Channel (PDC) logo and displaying various sponsor graphics, the silver aluminum supply drum sat tucked between two weathered boulders on the edge of a crater. The drum's upper rim, encircled by coloured LED's and various sensors, flashed when Sig got into visual proximity. Like the other drops over the previous days, the unit lay half buried under drifted sand.

Sig dug it out and thumbed the release latch, happy to see the door swing open without issue. The fine dust got into everything and tended to mess up the doors, even with their advanced magnetic seals. Each unit held water, food, power packs, oxygen, scrubber cartridges for her rebreather, and a tent that could be pressurized for sleeping. From the look of it, Devon had been running fast and light, barely denting the inventory.

The canister's sensor ring contained an array of cameras, kept clear by tiny compressed air jets. She'd watched the live footage from each one, watched Devon display his charms and provide a witty commentary. His helmet cam captured the run from his point of view, but the external shots were more epic and news worthy. In addition, the unit contained a personal diary recorder used for capturing notes and moments the duo hoped to compile into a behind the scenes feature for their adventure series. Devon hadn't stopped here for long, but Sig noticed that the recorder had been activated. He'd sent her a couple of private messages and she remembered this one. Fondly. Taking the opportunity for quick break, she sat down on a folding chair and patched in to watch it again.

"Sigrid. Baby. I thought I'd send you a personal message if I can figure out how upload directly to your account."

She could see tired eyes veiled behind his helmet visor and shifting suit membrane. He cracked a smile and winked.

"As the live streams sadly document, you can see this run is a terrible slog, mindless and repetitive. I'm not sure what I was expecting, but this wasn't it. Endless fields of red rock, sand dunes, dust traps, and blasted formations, a dull and unrelenting grind-fest. I should have started at the south-eastern escarpment like you wanted to, *that* would have been a challenge. Four days of following the transport track and I'm bored out of my skull. At least if you were here I'd have someone to annoy. Remember the time we first met, trapped on the summit of Mount Vinson for a week? You might have hated my jokes, but at least it passed the time."

It had been a hell of a first date. They'd both been climbing the mountain solo, from different sides, when a massive storm had rolled in. She'd hunkered down in her bombproof tent to be awakened by a half-frozen Yeti trying to get the zippers open.

"Who the hell are you?" she'd yelled, brandishing an ice axe.

"Devon," he wheezed, falling to his knees. "Devon Atherton. I summited via the... the eastern route but my tent. Lost. I saw you... I saw..." He tried to scrape the frost from his frozen face and slumped over, landing face first between her knees. The rest was history.

Sig un-paused the recording and watched his suit membrane turn cloudy, rippling and churning, before snapping back to transparency. A malfunction of some sort, she'd thought when she'd first watch the message, though nothing had shown up on the diagnostics.

Devon coughed. "Not sure if I'm pushing myself too hard or if I'm coming down with something. Phoebe says I'm fine, I'm just tired, but something's off. Hopefully I can hold myself together till I get up and down this rock."

He threw a kiss and fiddled with the camera controls. "For the record, I should never have listened to you. We should be doing this together, screw the cost and the PDC." He blinked, eyes glassy. "I miss you so much, just three more days to the top... three more. I'll send you another note when I get a chance. Love you!" The screen went dark with a fading curse.

"I love you too," she said to herself, pressing her helmet against her hands. The man possessed legendary networking skills and the almost magical ability to raise the amount of funds required for these kinds of expeditions, but he couldn't fix a toaster.

Another few hours of slow bounding put her into the roughest terrain yet, an area of collapsed lava tubes and steep ravines. She wasn't sure how Big Ben had managed to get through; it would have been a serious pain traversing around everything. She pushed herself to pick up the pace, skipping the next supply station by taking a dangerous, but direct route through the worst of it. Phoebe helped her navigate while providing a non-stop commentary about risk management. Sig didn't start listening until her rebreather and water supply reached dangerous levels, and the warning alerts became headache inducing. Her suit was amazing, using advanced mechanical counter pressure techniques to enable running and a military grade smart membrane to handle extreme environments, but it had its limits.

Phoebe piped up as Sig approached another dusty canister. "This drop's been giving warning signals. I don't think Devon closed the doors all the way and the works are likely all gummed up."

"Okay, I'll take a look."

The canister's doors appeared sealed but its sensor and proximity lights flashed red. Sig thumbed the release. Nothing happened. She pushed the button again. Still nothing.

"Phoebe, you there?"

"Of course."

"The doors won't open."

"Damn. Try the manual override."

Sig reached under the bottom of the doorframe and found the emergency lever. It was clogged with dust but popped out a couple of centimeters when she pulled on it. Then it jammed. She pulled harder. It gave another centimeter but stuck fast.

"The manual is jammed too."

"Maybe just skip it. The next drop is only three hours away if you push through the rough stuff."

"I thought I was the reckless one? I'd have to use up my entire reserve air supply to make that, or walk, and I can't spare the time. I'd rather refill here if possible. One more try."

Sig grabbed the lever with both hands, put her feet against the base of the canister, braced, and pulled hard. The lever resisted for a second before breaking off.

"Shit!"

Her arms snapped back and the pent-up energy tossed her up and away. On Earth, she would have just landed on her ass, but here, with the lesser gravity, she spun and flipped with a sort of awkward grace as she threw her hands out, landing atop a jagged outcrop. Sharp pain shot through her. Various displays began flashing red. Alarms blared.

"Sig! I'm reading a suit breach and damage to your air system. It's offline. Give me a status."

"The bloody lever broke and I took a tumble." She gasped, making matters worse. "Hold on, I–" The pain in her upper back spiked. She gasped again.

"You need to calm yourself. Your available air is down to 6% and dropping."

Sig closed her eyes and whispered her mantra. "Relax, release, ease. Relax, release, ease. Relax, release, ease."

"Better, but your suit hasn't sealed, I'm still reading a leak."

"I'm impaled on a sliver of rock." Sig wiggled, feeling spiked fingers of stone grind her ribs, clawing, scraping. "And I'm snagged." Panic. "Relax, release, ease."

"5%. Your reserve air control is giving an error, isn't it on a redundant circuit?"

"Yes."

"Damn, you need to get into the supply drop proto."

"I know!" Sig slid her hand under her back and tried to reach the toothy stone where it pierced her backpack, but the suit didn't provide the range of motion needed. Gel oozed, doing its best to keep the integrity intact, so she took a deep breath and rolled hard to the right. The suit tore but remained stuck. If anything, the fingers of stone penetrated deeper, gripped tighter. She rolled to the left. The suit tore again, alarms shrieking. Let me go dammit! She screamed and slammed herself forward as hard as she could, ripping herself from the rock and face planting into the ground.

"3%. The supply drop. Now!"

Praying the membrane could seal the hole, she gritted her teeth and crawled." I know, I know, but I can't seem to get into the damn thing."

"Well, you have to."

Sig collapsed in front of the blinking capsule. What the hell was she doing out here?

FOUR DAYS AGO

Nestled in her cot, Sig listened to the background hum of the Base and thought about Devon. A week earlier he'd been snuggled next to her, snoring, the way he always did after one of his blitzkrieg style training sessions. He'd crawl into bed, cuddle a bit, and fall asleep, his arm splayed across her body. A nice arm. She loved his tattoos, especially the stylized bug-eyed monster acquired during his days in the marines. At least they hadn't come across one of *those* here.

She thought about the problem, attacked it analytically like she attacked everything. Olympus Mons was massive, but not technically difficult. The route they'd selected meandered three hundred and fifty kilometers through manageable terrain. A lot of elevation gain, three times Everest, but not steep given the vast distance.

A seven-day trip, fifty kilometers per day, with a supply canister every twenty-five kilometers. Easy math.

Sig flew through the corridors and burst into the Commander's quarters, kicking his bed and jarring him awake.

"I'm going to run it."

The Commander squinted, raising his hand up to block out the sudden light. "Absolutely not. Are you crazy?"

"Andre, listen to me, I can do this. Yes, it's risky, but it's the only way."

"You think you can run up a twenty-kilometer-high mountain solo, in the middle of a major blow, find your boy, and bring him down? No support. No contingency. In the Armée de l'Air we call that a suicide mission."

"I designed my suit to handle the worst Mars can throw at it. I'm in the best shape of my life. Except for the final unit, the supply drops are all there and functional. I could leave now and be at the top in five days if I push it."

"I thought you were sick?" The Commander swung his legs over the edge of the bed and cracked his neck.

"I'm better."

"Like hell you are."

"I'm mostly better. Ask Phoebe."

He grunted and rolled out of bed. "You remind me of my wife, stubborn as hell." He looked at her determined face. Sighed. "Get your gear together and get some rest. I'll recharge the rover and drive you as far as I can."

❖❖❖

Never, ever, give up. She was going to get to the top of this damned mountain, find Devon, and get him down. Get both of them down. Alive.

Lights ringing the supply canister flashed, crimson eyes dancing in sequence. Laughing. Laughing at her. A never-ending repeating pattern. Screw linear thinking, she thought, time for a direct solution.

"2%." There was a hysterical edge to Phoebe's voice.

Sig pulled herself to her feet, found a nearby spear of rock, and gave it a good kick with the soul of her boot. It shivered. She backed up and took a running leap, nailing it with both feet. The outcrop cracked, snapped off. Sig picked it up and smashed against the canister's door latch. "Open, you damn thing!" The latch deformed and pieces broke away. Another. And another. The fourth strike cracked the door open, revealing the precious supplies inside. Sig flung the rock into the storm and screamed, brute force *can* win over ingenuity. Devon would be proud.

Phoebe sighed with relief. "You done scaring the hell out of me?"

Sig grabbed an air cylinder, mated the valve to the emergency adapter on her collar, and flooded her helmet. Took a deep breath. "For now, at least."

Wiggling into her inflating survival tent a few minutes later, she unstrapped her life support unit and unwound by taking apart the damaged back plate, switching her brain from mortality to engineering. Such a major design flaw passing all the air circulation in parallel near a single point, a failure that almost killed her. She wanted to kick herself, or cry, or both, but she found her focus and examined the oxygen regulator control conduit. Strange, she'd expected it to be punctured, but it looked crushed, like someone had grabbed it and squeezed. At least her gel membrane hadn't fouled the components. After watching Devon's membrane's odd behaviour and suspecting contamination, she'd spent a couple of days tuning hers, reprogramming it to reject all foreign material, especially ultra-fine Martian dust. That last thing she needed was malfunctioning life support.

Once she was satisfied with her patch job, she lay back and tried to rest. One hundred kilometers remained, a day and half at her present pace, if she could sustain it. If her body, suit, and most importantly, her mind held up. She worried about her mind the most, it wouldn't take much to slip into a dark space and never return.

❖❖❖

Twelve kilometers. Ten kilometers. Sig's mind wasn't the first to go. Her body screamed, legs, hips and back an aching mess, her lungs chunky and voice hoarse. The slow, bounding gait she'd adopted worked well in the Martian gravity, but three hundred and fifty kilometers was still a hell of a long way to run uphill, in a spacesuit, in five days. She was at the point where she constantly checked her location, estimated, of course, with the storm interfering with GPS, and watched her destination grow ever closer. Nine kilometers. Eight kilometers. Seven. Run a bit, walk a bit, run more, walk. Almost there, she told herself, almost there.

A fractured ridge took her to the summit. Dust swirled, plumes billowing while raw electricity crackled, playing havoc with sensors and communication systems. Faces in the dust. Voices on the wind. Not that Mars had wind, not enough air pressure, especially at this altitude. Still, she kept picking up faint whispers on her long-range com, whispers she hoped were Devon's. Base, however, claimed electrical interference.

Two kilometers. One kilometer. Five hundred meters. One hundred meters. She gained the high point at last, the massive caldera of the volcano dropping away below her, the epic view blocked by suspended dust. A massive bolt of lightning illuminated the ridge and more bolts flickered nearby. The heart of the storm. Sig unslung and dropped the makeshift sack of gear she'd scavenged from the previous drop and checked her chronometer. Five Days, six hours and seventeen minutes. She'd beaten the planetary record by more than a day. Devon's record.

"Phoebe, I made it. Mostly dead, but I'm there." Her voice was little more than a rasp.

No response.

"Tarkis Orbital Station? Hellas Colony?"

Nothing.

A round of diagnostics couldn't find a technical problem so it must be interference from the storm. Annoying and enlightening, it explained the lack of communication from Devon, though it wouldn't have taken him long to move down mountain and out of the affected region. With that thought nagging her mind she explored the area. No sign of the supply drop. No blinking sensor lights. No reflective aluminum. Not even the transport tracks. Was she lost? Had she gone off course? That didn't seem possible. She scrambled around. "Devon? Where are you?" Empty air.

When she found the hole - an ominous fissure five meters long and two across - understanding flooded in. The entire ridge was a veneer covering a subsurface honeycombed with lava tubes and tunnels.

"Phoebe, you see this?" Still nothing.

Sig secured a length of ultra-light, ultra-thin climbing silk to a jutting outcrop, clipped in, and wiggled to the edge of the hole. Crappy visibility as always, the dust scattering her light. Rolling onto her back, she closed her eyes and tried to push away the fog that clouded her mind. He had to be down there. Had to be. She slid over the edge and rappelled to the bottom. Twelve meters below, the final supply drop sat half buried in rock fall, on its side, doors hanging open. She searched the immediate area for Devon, tried every communication band available. Dust, darkness, and silence. Three rough tunnels led off in different directions.

Back to the drop. A wreck, the sensor ring shattered, internals a tangled mess. All the supplies had been removed, a positive sign that the fall hadn't killed him, but where was he? The primary communication unit had been pulled out, worked on, and stuffed back in, still broken, but the recording unit, semi-independent and nothing more than a glorified camera, activated with a bit of prodding. One recording.

Devon's haggard face, obscured by a cracked and tape patched faceplate, filled the monitor. "Sig, I know you'll get this, if anyone can get up here and save my butt, it'll be you. I'm sorry I let you– everyone down. You always said my antics would be the death of me. I know you weren't entirely serious, but you were prophetic in this case. One huge Martian victory jump and the ground went out from under me. I guess that old lava tube was just waiting to swallow the first person dumb enough run up here."

She paused the playback, a tiny laugh catching in her throat. His signature move, leaping into the air and clicking his heals at the end of every race, the top of every mountain. Dumb ass.

"The fall broke my legs, internal bleeding, the works, and life support system is having a rough time. I hope the suit can keep me alive long enough for you to get here." He half-grinned, more a grimace than anything. "Do you remember Cameron Phillips? My old buddy at Teragon Mining Corp? I got word they'll provide access to the ice shaft they're drilling on Europa. PDC will fund your idea for a diving expedition. It might take a few years to plan and build gear for, but it's happening! Twenty kilometers down. Can you imagine? Anyways, forget Vesta for now, I'm sure you have some great ideas for what we'll need." He touched his faceplate against the camera and rolled over, dry hacking. "Sig. Sigrid. I'm sorry. I love you so much. Try not to hate me."

Knowing that it wouldn't help but not caring, she gave the unit a hard smack. Piece of junk, she'd have to fix it after she fueled and calmed down. She hated this, hated not knowing if he was dead or alive.

Devon had to be around here somewhere. Shining her light into every nook and cranny, it didn't take long to find the marks, numbers scratched into the walls at calf height at the start of each of the tunnels. Number three had an arrow next to it, the intent obvious. This way, it screamed, this way.

After a long scramble through the debris filled lava tube, Sig came across signs of a recent disturbance. Rocks cleared out of the way, a depleted power pack, and an aluminum strut, part of the supply canister's internal frame. It had been used as a digging tool, the end scratched and worn. Then she saw it, the pressure tent, its blue mesh half deflated, positioned below a chimney narrow enough for a strong climber to shimmy up.

"Devon?" she whispered, "Are you there?" Dead air. She didn't pick up any movement or heat. Damn. For better or worse she had to know. Sig opened the tiny airlock and wiggled in. Once it sealed, and it did seal thank god, she opened the half inflated main compartment. Devon lay there in his suit and helmet, on his back, unmoving, his legs splinted with aluminum struts and bound with repair tape. A thick layer of discoloured bio-gel coated the outside of his suit and the supply canister's missing contents lay spread around in haphazard piles.

The last corpse she'd seen was on Everest, a climber crushed by a rock fall with only his legs and red double boots protruding from the rubble. A grim sight, she'd kept her distance. Here, within the confines of the tent, it was close and unavoidable. A coffin. Devon's faceplate was gelled and frosted over so she couldn't see his face, a small favour, and she reached out and held his hand. Gave it a little squeeze. "I don't hate you."

There was a squeeze back. Sig jerked away and watched as his hand twitched. She fumbled for her patch cable, scraped gel from a port, and plugged it into his suit, feeding it power. "Dev?"

Alive. Mostly dead, maybe, but alive. She wanted to scream, wanted to throw herself on top of him, but she started working on his life support unit, coaxing it from nothing to minimal. It didn't read as operational, flat lines across the board, but the computer lied. Mostly dead wasn't all dead. No way. She felt tears trickle down her face to be carried off by the reclamation system. "Try not to make this a habit. Rescues are a lot of work you know."

The frozen suit warmed and he continued twitching, a spark of life somewhere down deep. The gel membrane, a deep rusty red, looked wrong. Why was it on the outside of the suit? Had he reprogrammed it for some specific purpose? She pulled what she could from his computer. She'd analyze it when she had a spare moment.

"I'll get you out of here, don't worry. I'll carry you, if I have to. Once we can get back down to the next supply dump or two, it should get easier." Maybe she could just pull the tent behind her, a crude sled. It would be a bumpy, uncomfortable ride and the laminated shell would shred, but it should work.

Plans churning in her mind, Sig slithered out of the tent and made her way to the supply dump. First on the agenda, let Base know the good news. While Devon didn't have the skill to repair the big com unit, she did. Its signal couldn't penetrate the rock, so up the rope she went, hauling it behind her, back into the endless storm. Dust. Lightning. Her sack of scavenged gear wasn't where she thought she'd left it. Damn, she was too tired to deal with that right now. She plunked herself on a flat boulder and plugged the communicator into her suit's power supply. Not optimal, but would have to do. The unit powered up and found a signal right away. "Sig? Sigrid? Is that you? Do you copy?"

"Phoebe! Thank god."

"Finally, we've been trying to get through for hours, had a lot of electrical interference so we switched to one of the military satellites with a lot more power. What's your status?"

"I found Devon. He fell into a deep fissure, messed himself up something fierce. I'm just making plans to get him down."

"That's fantastic!" Phoebe yelled something and Sig heard muted cheering in the background. "I have excellent news. The footage from your rescue... yes, we recorded what we could... has pumped PDC's ratings so far up that they've bribed... asked the military to try and land a shuttle outside of the storm's center. Think you can manage thirty more kilometers? Tomorrow?"

Recorded everything? Damn, she didn't even want to think about that. "When? I'm a wreck. I'll have to drag him." The thought of running further cut her soul. She needed to sleep for a week, a month, but the sooner she got Devon to medical facilities, the better chance he had. She couldn't fool herself thinking he was out of the woods yet.

"Yes. We'll start at first light."

"Excellent, I'll let them know."

"Thanks, I'd better go check on him. Talk to you shortly."

"Take care and great job, I knew you could do it."

Sig unplugged, stood up, and stretched. So much to do, so little time. Now where did she stash those supplies? Her power packs needed a recharge and air system a scrubber cartridge sooner than later. Something moved at the edge of her vision. A faint shadow. Devon. He staggered out of the swirling dust, from the direction of the caldera, and stopped, the contaminated bio-gel covering his suit in a deep red, almost black, patchwork skin.

"Dev. You shouldn't be on your feet. You're still mostly dead." How was he on his feet? Mobile? For that matter, how the hell did he get up here? She'd used the climbing thread to pull up the communicator.

He swayed, didn't say anything, just stood, faceplate so thick with gel she couldn't see his face.

"Dev? Talk to me. What's going on?"

He lifted one boot, struggled to balance, and slammed his heel onto the communication unit, smashing it to pieces. Sig bounced over and pushed him back.

"What the hell? Don't... we need that. What–"

He shoved hard and Sig flew backwards, catching herself with her hands as she struck the ground. She watched Devon stomp the unit into unfixable fragments. The gel gushed, thick and energetic. A serious malfunction. He must be out of his mind, delusional. "Devon. Honey. Stop please, let me help you."

Devon stopped, stepped over to her, bending down until his helmet almost touched hers. "You need to get off those broken legs," she said, taking a deep breath and reaching out, touching his faceplate, scraping away the gel.

Dead eyes stared out from a withered, mummified face.

She screamed, ripping her hand away. Tried to at least. Gel flowed over her glove and up her arm. Binding. Trapping. It reached the cuff seal and started eating its way through, her suit indicating a sudden loss of integrity. Thoughts and possibilities flashed through her mind, none plausible. This shouldn't be, couldn't be. The gel, while semi-intelligent, had limited capabilities. Animating a corpse wasn't one of them, or hadn't been. She grabbed Devon's, or what had been Devon's, shoulder with her free hand and tried to kick off against his chest. Both hand and foot became entangled as more gel oozed out of every seal in his suit. Her weight overbalanced him and they toppled the ground.

Get away, her mind screamed, whatever it was, it had killed Devon and she was next. The gel started working on her other glove seal and flowed up her boot. Think. Think! She'd suspected the membranes could be susceptible to microscopic particulate matter but there had been no evidence that dust could disrupt or damage the encoded A.I. Maybe it degraded, mutated it over time? Her own membrane was programmed to be far more resilient, to reject all foreign material. Reject and expel.

Maybe that was the solution. She stopped fighting and let the gel worm it's way into her glove seal, ignoring the screeching of her suit's integrity alarm. Devon's membrane touched hers and stopped. Devon shuddered. His gel writhed, recoiling, letting go.

Sig rolled away and stood up, panting. Get the hell out of here, her mind screamed as Devon climbed to his feet and lumbered towards her. As much as it hurt, she needed to get up and run.

❖❖❖

"... run."

Sig opened her eyes, artificial light piercing her grime-coated visor. G-forces pulled at her prone body and she felt numb, the distinctive numbness of painkillers, and cold; her suit wrapping her like a coffin. Where? The shuttle? She'd made it then, gotten down from the summit, found the LZ, escaped the nightmare.

A relieved "Thank heaven," came out a croaked, "Th..."

A hand wiped away the dust obscuring her vision and a dark angular helmet hovered, blocking the harsh light. "Excellent, you're awake. Take a drink if you can."

She took a long pull from her water dispenser and tried to rise, struggling against invisible bonds.

"Easy now. You're strapped in aboard the One-Eyed Jack, a Colonial Marine drop ship deployed from the *USS Paxton*. I'm Corporal Banks. Medic."

"Thank... Thank you Corporal." Stone on stone, she cleared her throat and drank more. "I didn't think I'd make it."

"You almost didn't. We were just about to give up when Lieutenant Atherton walked out of the dust, carrying you over his shoulder, and dropped you into my arms without saying a goddamn word. Retired or not, he's still one hell of a marine."

Lieutenant Atherton. Devon? Rescue? Dead eyes bored into hers. An angry Mars rose up, grasping, pulling her down into oblivion. "But... Devon's dead." Or worse.

"Ha. Sure, he looked dead, his suit a patchwork of tape and leaky gel, but so did you. He's up in the cockpit with the Captain. We're taking you both to the Paxton, best medical facilities in the fleet, they'll have you on your feet in no—" Banks coughed, shook his head. "Sorry, I'm not... not feeling great. Coming down with a cold I think."

Cold. Her mind twisted, seeing dead eyes again, dead cold eyes. Faces. Nightmares. None of it real, none of it possible, just twisted hallucinations from a mind pushed past the edge. Devon was alive. Alive. A sob escaped her throat and she shivered.

"I can't do anything about the chill sadly, your bio-membrane was damaged and erratic when he brought you in. Blocked access to your ports. I had to disable it and flush it out. It fought me till the end, unwilling to leave your suit, unwilling to leave you. Never seen anything like it."

Flush it out? That explained the cold, coffin feeling. The membrane had been her second skin for a week. She felt naked without it. Vulnerable.

Banks coughed again, harder this time. His helmet shook. A line of deep red appeared across the bottom of his visor, thick gel oozing out and running down his chin and dribbling onto hers. It slid through her suit seals as she strained to escape the straps holding her down, flowed over her face as she screamed.

5

The Fourth Horseman

J ack made a graceful arc, crashing through a pile
of wooden crates and onto a collapsible whiskey
barrel. Despite the set's shoddy construction, a
splinter caught his back and dug in, tearing his
duster and opening stitches from the previous day.

"I'm too old for this shit," he groaned.

The bar room window gaped behind him, the
slivers forming a serrated smile. One falling wedge
exploded near his head, peppering him with sugar
glass, while Kid Curry pushed through the
swinging doors of the saloon and adjusted his hat.
A dark halo surrounded the big man, something
out of the negative zone, and Jack knew his past
had caught up with him.

"You're making this too easy Jack. Where's the
fire I've heard so much about? All burnt out?"

A terrible pun, but it was a 'B' movie. He leapt to his feet and reached for his pistol. The Colt wasn't in its holster.

"Looking for this?" The outlaw held up the .45 and admired the engraving on the grip. "You fancy the buffalo? When I'm done with you, you'll be as extinct as they are."

Jack winced. Who wrote this crap? Still, he'd have to play along until he could figure out which demon possessed the actor and what he could do about it. "I thought we was friends, Kid? You, me, Sam, Butch, the whole gang. Why yah doing this?"

The Kid tossed him the revolver. "Elfie's my girl. Mine! She said you were looking at her, all misty like. Now on your feet you no good layabout, it's time to die like a man."

"CUT!" Darren, the second unit director on 'The Wild Bunch Rides Again', walked over and helped Jack up. "Nice to see you put your back into it. I'm thinking one more take, this time from down the street." He yelled and the crew appeared. "Let's get this mess cleaned up."

George Carver, playing Curry, cleared his throat and smoothed down his walrus mustache. "Jack and I have to settle up first. I meant it about Elfie. I don't brook any second-rate outlaw fawning over my girl." His eyes burned with inner light, feral and menacing.

"Nice improv George," said Darren, "but we're on break. Save it for the next take."

The shot was a thunderclap and Darren looked surprised as the red stain spider webbed across his abdomen. The director collapsed with a gurgle.

"Holy shit!" someone yelled as the crew screamed and ran. Jack looked around for a weapon that wasn't a cheap tin prop, but stopped when he felt the barrel of George's Schofield poking his ribs.

"Hold up old friend. It's time to see just how fast 'Black Jack' Ketchum really is."

Jack's mind raced. He'd retired, left the service of the Almighty, hung up his guns, his real guns, and with his rugged good looks, found a job, and a life, in Hollywood. He should have known it wouldn't be that easy.

George motioned with his revolver.

Brett, a sound technician and apparently fearless, lunged from behind a thick post and tackled the stocky actor. Laughing, George shrugged him off and shot him point blank, splashing his brains across the gravel.

"Your turn Jack. Don't worry, it'll be a fair fight."

Jack checked his revolver. It wasn't a prop after all, the cylinder held real shells. He knew his adversary now, only the demon warrior Leraje would be so arrogant, and so confident, to suggest a fair duel. Easy enough. He pulled the duster back, holstered the Colt, and waited. Leraje smiled, flickering, an aura of darkness rising to form twisted ephemeral wings.

"Draw!"

They both fired and time slowed. Jack watched his bullet catch Leraje in the heart, the demon bursting apart in an explosion of black smoke. His satisfaction was short lived, however, as a hell forged slug punched through his own left shoulder, cold fire searing his immortal soul. His knees buckling, he fell against a green screen and tried to steady himself, but his arm went through the canvas. Cheap set, he thought to himself, as he slid through, expecting to land hard. The floor came and went.

A blast of hot sand caught him in the face, sticking to oozing sweat. He brushed it away and looked out onto a bright, golden desert. Four horses and three riders shimmered in the heat. The closest rider tipped her wide brimmed hat and tossed him the reins of a massive black charger.

"Took your time," she said, pointing to empty saddle. "We've been waiting. Mount up."

"Where am I?"

"Everywhere. Nowhere. Just understand that you're needed and you've been recalled. There's trouble brewing. Big trouble."

Jack nodded, rubbed his healing shoulder, and swung himself up onto the horse. Another day, another world, another mission. "Who has my sword?"

6

Dead Reckoning

Dead. Again. One minute I'm following an easy mark, the next I'm face down in the gutter, pulsing blood courtesy of the world's largest hand cannon. Why hadn't I looked both ways before crossing the street? Lotus blossoms and delicate curves, lots and lots of curves. Even incorporeal I can smell the flowers, their phantom fragrance returning me to the pricy boutique hotel room from last night. A little piece of heaven, the closest I'll ever get.

An engine roars, tires squeal, and a black SUV speeds off, rear lights vanishing into the evening drizzle like the last moments of a dying Marlboro. No plates. No identifying features. Not even a scratch. It's a Beamer, though, which implies assholes. Calgary is full of assholes, so tracking them down will be next to impossible. I'll find a way though, I always do. Finding's what I'm good at, what folks pay me the big bucks for. When I'm alive of course, being dead makes it harder.

Clinging to the mortal realm as a shade, I watch my perforated body twitch, watch my life drain into a culvert with the dirty rain, more dead meat in a town built off the backbone of the cattle industry. Cowtown. Oil money wraps the crumbling sandstone in a pretty new skin of steel and glass, but deep down it's still the Wild West.

The well-dressed mark I'd been following slinks out of the shadows and nudges his wingtips into my oozing ribcage. Arnie Gerste, small time import-export broker and self-important wise guy. He kneels down and goes through my pockets. Beer Money. Phone. Car Keys. I curse when he lifts the keys, curse louder when he strolls down the street, spinning the fob on his finger and pausing every so often to press the alarm.

I want to kick his ass, take back my stuff, but I'm scraped thin, a soul flapping in the ether. The Beamer loops back and stops, disgorging a Neanderthal who opens the rear door for the second-rate gangster. They argue about a car, my car. It gets heated. Arnie climbs in, rolls down the window, and continues clicking the fob as they drive off.

I'd follow but I can't, I'm bound to my body and don't get ten feet before the tether drags me back. More metaphysical bullshit. The cheap watch on my limp, outstretched arm ticks. 9:04 PM. Three hours to complete the job, three hours to save the world, three hours to get the girl. I plunk myself on the curb, lean against a rusting fire hydrant, and wait for the cavalry.

What feels like ages later, a black hearse roars out shadows and pulls up. It's a modified Jaguar E class, all shiny chrome and deep black gloss, a huge step up from the usual Guild shit-can I expect. A slight, robed figure gets out, glides over to my remains, and sets down a red enameled toolbox embellished with the device of a laughing skull, one eye socket cavernous, the other, tiny.

"What happened to the Caddy?" I ask, dragging myself to my feet. "Did your mouldy old boss finally lose control of the purse strings?"

The figure, a priestess of Khenti-Amentiu, doesn't reply. They never do. It's the same every time: I poke, they ignore me, I poke harder, and they give me the eye. One of these days I'll get them talking, find out what's under those robes.

"A slight, robed figure gets out, glides over to my remains,
and sets down a red enamelled toolbox . . ."

In my dreams it's Aphrodite, in my nightmares it's scarabs, asps, and scorpions.

No harm in trying, though, what's the worst that could happen? "We should go for a drink one night. I'm sure I owe you a few hundred by now."

She gives me the cold shoulder and produces a ledger, tosses it at me, hieroglyphs twinkling on the cover. A name. My name.

I snatch it out of the air, flip it open, and run my spectral finger down the page. "I have three lives on account." Or not. "Two? Oh right, Christmas Eve." Poisoned absinthe. Quick, painless, and forgettable as murderous deaths go.

At the bottom, a crimson thumbprint glows. I touch it and watch the tally drop to one. One bloody life left. The closer I get to the final swan song, the harder it is to return to the mortal coil. I'll need to get more; it's long past time to put some quarters into the machine.

Tucking the book into her robe, the priestess kneels and opens the box. It unfolds like a flower, compartmentalized drawers bursting with arcane instruments. Nice trick. She selects a silver ankh and probes the hole where my chest used to be, gets it good and gooey, flicks some blood into the air. A hazy image of my body appears, all Vitruvian

Man'ish, the damaged parts black and ugly. I'm heartless, but I knew that already.

"So, about that drink. There's a quaint little club tucked away on First Street that brings in Sakara Gold, a little taste of the old country. Interested?"

The eye. I knew it was coming, but the hourglass stare forces a chill down my spine. Time to shut up and let her get down to business. She sits cross-legged before my body and plays an eerie note on a rune-encrusted bone flute. Human bone, no doubt, the guild acolytes have all the best toys. The note becomes a song, rhythmic and soothing, forcing a cloud of golden fog to coalesce and settle into the bullet holes. My soul flows back into my body, moving at the speed of life, to crash into the wall between this world and the next. Crashing it, smashing it, and punching through in a wild surge of fire and light.

❖❖❖

When I open my eyes I'm alone on the street, coughing and spitting out bits of something resembling cotton candy. I hate the stuff; it sticks to my teeth and coats the inside of my mouth like cheap granular sugar. Worse yet, my back hurts when I bend over to hack. No matter how much I complain, beg, or bribe, they always put me back together the way I was when this whole adventure started. I'm cursed to spend an eternity bitching about it.

Sirens blare, heading in my direction, providing impetus to get a move on. It's not a busy street, less so with the rain, but someone's heard the shots and called it in. I'm blocks away when I realize I've left my hat. "Goddamn." I consider turning around, but it's just a cheap Goodwill felt, not a Borsalino or anything. Screw it. With a quick check to make sure I'm not being followed, I duck into the Lord Nelson.

The light is turned so far down I stop to let my eyes adjust. I miss the old days, when it was legal to smoke indoors, and you could cut the murk in here with a sword. Now they compensate by keeping it as dim as possible to hide the frightening seventies décor and scarier clientele. Rick is working the bar, so I head that way, intent on a stiff drink to get the candy taste out of my mouth before I give my client the bad news.

I'm too slow and a slim arm pulls me into a shadow filled booth. Lien Hua. She drapes herself over me, arms sliding around my neck like a couple of velvet snakes, before she recoils in disgust. "Ugh, you smell like death."

"You have no idea. It's been a rough evening."

She notices my perforated, blood soaked shirt, and shredded trench coat. Runs a finger through the holes, traces a pair of old scars that traverse my chest. "I see. You *look* like death. Did you find Gerste? We don't have much time."

"We were about to have a heart-to-heart when his guardian angels showed up."

A fork goes deep into the tabletop and sticks there, quivering. "You lost him? After all that work..."

"Not quite, the bastard slipped up and stole my phone. I'm on my way to the office to trace it."

She relaxes. A little. "Good. It's critical we learn where Gerste made that delivery. A dark presence nears, powerful and dangerous. I'll lend you my strength in case there's any more unexpected trouble." She crinkles her nose and cuddles back up. I feel a hand on my thigh.

"Whoa princess, none of that now. I'm not sure how old you are, but it isn't old enough."

"That's not what you said last night." She snuggles closer.

Last night? I conjure up some elusive memories. Jazz? Tea? A pillow-top mattress at Hotel Elan? Terminal trauma tends to mess with my mind, cheese graters the short-term, but it all floods back in a rush of sounds and smells. "True." A lot had been said, little of it verbal. "But I need to get moving. We can celebrate after I find your honourable ancestor."

A pout and an exaggerated sigh. "Of course, you're right. Nothing's more important than freeing Master Wu. If you can't release him before midnight, he'll be trapped for another hundred years." She strokes her phone and brings up the time. "That leaves you two and a half hours."

"To find the thing..." Another fragmented memory.

"Not a thing, a Mandarin relic. It'll be in a casket marked with the Han character for ginseng." She draws a 參 on a napkin pushes it into my hand.

Ah yes, that's right, an ancient Chinese casket. In a town bursting with cowboy collectables, it should stick out like a sore thumb.

The princess hops over my lap, slides out of the booth, and pulls on a heavy overcoat. She pauses to run her hand through my matted hair and I groan as she grabs a handful and yanks me up off the bench, kissing me hard enough leave scorch marks. Electric warmth wraps me in a comforting, protective blanket.

"I'm a lot older than I look," she purrs before vanishing into the gloom, leaving the air thick with the scent of flowers on a rainy day.

❖❖❖

A quick trip to the bar, a beer that goes down faster than a hooker on Third Street, and a coffee to go. My office is an old brownstone, tucked above the mouldering ruin of an independent bookstore forced out of business by the big chains. I notice the landlord's boarded up the broken windows again. Not sure why anyone would want to squat in a hole full of water damaged horror novels and vengeful ghosts, but this town has all kinds.

The outside light turns on as I drag myself up three flights of stairs, and I smell the fresh spray paint before I see the metallic stencil on the door. 'Lust and Pound.' Dammit, tagged by lowlife scum *again*. Once this job is wrapped up I going to hang around with a baseball bat and nip that in the bud. It's tiresome *and* expensive. I use my bloody sleeve to fix the o and the F.

My office, a converted studio apartment, is a mess, chaos and entropy trumping all semblance of order. I trail my fingers along battered paperbacks jammed into wall-to-wall bookshelves and trip over a pile of Amazon boxes I'd meant to break down and recycle months ago. The books are my treasures, pulp fiction gems collected through multiple lifetimes. I plop down at my desk and pick up my latest find, a rare first edition of Edgar Rice Burroughs's Synthetic Men of Mars. Synthetic, exactly how I feel after being taken apart and put back together.

Locating my laptop under a pile of last week's newspapers, I fire up Find My Phone, praying Gerste hadn't turned it off. He hasn't and it shows up in the old community of Ramsay, right across the river. I make a call on my landline.

"Yes?"

"Rags, it's Boone. I'm looking for your boy, Bjorn. A quick muscle job with good money in it."

"Tagger, this is a bad time."

"Sorry, but it's a matter of life and death."

"Always, but he's busy." Echoing gunshots fill the background. "Why don't you try Galan, I hear he's back from Barcelona. Said he was hitting the strip tonight."

"Thanks, appreciated."

Galan Arlington, aka Galan Hammerhand. The son of a bitch is a hard-drinking, skirt-chasing, kneecapping bundle of trouble. An old friend, one that owes me big time.

A quick car-to-go and I find Galan at the Drum and Monkey, his booming voice and twisting laugh echoing into the street. I have sober second thoughts. Did I need this kind of crazy? I brush the doubt aside and push through the drunks crowding the door. There he is, all three and half feet, standing on the end of the bar in a fancy tux, holding a terrified suit by the front of his shirt. The guy's feet dangle in midair.

Galan gives me a quick glance. "Boone! Long time old man. Still dressing like a friendless vagabond. Don't you have any pride? Let me take you shopping, I know this righteous tailor."

"I might have to take up on that, but I'm in a hurry and I need that favour. Have a minute?"

The dwarf smashes his forehead into the man's nose, splattering it in an explosion of blood and cartilage. Dropping the screaming fellow in a crumpled heap, he hops down, and yanks a gold ring off the guy's hand. Pockets it. "Sure, but I have to catch a flight in–" He looks at his jewel encrusted Rolex. "–116 minutes."

"This shouldn't take long. I need to collect some intel for a client. It's over in Ramsay."

"Sounds fun. Wait here, I'll grab my ride."

He disappears around back and pulls up in a glistening red Italian roadster. I whistle. "Maserati Spyder? Nice."

"It's all about image, Boone, one day you'll figure that out."

We hop across the river and along the bluff overlooking the Stampede grounds. This part of Ramsay is nicer than I remember, the tiny bungalows replaced with expensive infills and duplexes. Gentrification. My Mustang sits along the curb, in front of an ultra-modern two-story with long, narrow windows and corrugated green steel trim. The familiar black Beamer is parked in the driveway.

"The guy I need is in there, covered by a couple of meat-heads."

Galan shrugs, unconcerned. "You want them alive?"

"Not really, they killed me earlier."

"Again? Dammit Boone, you die more than a 1985 Yugo. At this rate, you'll never be able to retire."

"Yeah, yeah."

Still shaking his head, he hands me his jacket, picks up a rock, and creeps over to the BMW. The rock goes through the passenger window and the alarm blares. Before you can say boo, two identical slabs of beef in black suits charge out of the house. The first one hefts a pistol with a bore like a train tunnel. "Kid, what the hell are you doing?" He grabs Galan's shoulder and spins him around, eyes widening when realizes his mistake.

The dwarf flashes a twenty-four carat grin and punches him in the groin. Hard. The stunned goon sees stars and falls to his knees retching, chest heaving. Galan runs up the side of the SUV, spins through the air, and plants his polished leather shoes into the side of the man's head. The thug hits the dirt hard enough to cause a tremor.

The second goon backs away, digging for his own weapon. Galan, still airborne and moving, tucks, rolls, and scythes through his knees in a whirlwind of bone-crunching fury. As the thug falls back howling, the dwarf walks up the man's collapsing body, flings himself into the air, and twists in slow motion as the pull of gravity drops his elbow onto the goon's throat. The sound is terrible, like a bat hitting a side of beef.

Twenty seconds. Maybe.

Kicking the gun into the bushes, Galan finds the keys and turns off the car alarm, straightens his shirt, and cracks his neck.

"Thanks Boone, just what the doctor ordered."

"Glad I could provide the evening's entertainment. Those Chuck Norris action jeans?"

"Ha! You wish. They haven't made those for twenty-five years. Miguel Caballero Black all the way."

"As good as they say?"

He heads for the open door. "None better. Come hang with me in Barcelona and I'll set you up." The well-appointed entryway contains a shoe rack holding a stack of purple crocs and a pair of freshly polished wingtips. Galan picks up the shoes and rubs the leather. Shakes his head with distain. "Cheap knockoffs." Baseball caps and rain jackets hang from coat hooks and a dripping umbrella leans in the corner. Strains of Hockey Night in Canada bounce down the hall.

Arnie hunches forward on a rich leather recliner, watching the game in black silk pajamas, a prissy ascot, and another pair of purple crocs. A regular fashion statement. Pabst Blue Label cans crowd a coffee table and he drains the one in hand when the hardwood creaks. "Schultz, grab me a beer on your way in. This overtime is killing me."

"No can-do poser. Where do you shop? The Salvation Army?"

The man drops his beer can, rises, and notices me behind the dwarf. "You. You're dead!"

"I get that a lot."

"You took seven bullets. The holes—"

I pull open my coat and tap my chest.

"But..." His brain isn't processing what he sees, what he remembers.

"Speaking of funerals, your boys are eating dirt out front, start talking or you'll be joining them. Where did you deliver that package this afternoon?"

Arnie clams up and starts inching backwards towards a bookshelf, eyes on a Glock tucked between a Wayne Gretzky bobble head and a porcelain Jesus. He doesn't get far. Galan does a little flip and puts both feet into his groin, smashing him to the floor. The man goes white, croaks out a feeble "Fuck you," and staggers up, still intent on the gun.

"Do you have a grudge against testicles or something? Don't kill him before he can answer my damn question!"

Galan isn't listening. He launches himself off the ottoman, gets his legs around the Arnie's neck, and uses his weight to spin the flailing man in a complete three-sixty. The wannabe gangster crashes through the coffee table, cans spinning across the room. Galan grabs Arnie's throat and squeezes.

"The nice hobo asked you a question."

Arnie gurgles.

"I can't hear you." Galan squeezes harder.

Arnie chokes out a name. "Slate Resources. But if he—"

"Yes, yes, if he finds out you talked, he's going to kill you." Galan slams the man's head into the floor until both are dented. "Not going to be a problem."

It's grim enough that I turn away. Not that I have any sympathy, the bastard killed me and stole my car, but ugly is ugly.

"There you go Boone, nothing to it."

"Thanks."

"Of course, what are friends for? Not sure you want to get into it with Nathaniel Slate though. The man's a treacherous psychopath with a long reach."

"You know him?"

"We've done business."

"I don't have much choice. It's a paying job with fringe benefits."

Galan nods and scratches his head. "A word. Keep an eye out for hired help. Last I heard Slate had a hot little Russian throat slitter on payroll."

"Tatyana Rurikovich?"

"That's the one."

"She's dead, ran into the Totoro Sisters last month and went home in a box."

"Really?" He shakes his head. "What a shame. He'll have hired someone else by now though, so watch your back."

"I will."

"Oh, and one more thing." The dwarf flashes another smile and pulls out a thick billfold, peeling off a few high denomination bills and tucking them into my pocket. "Please," he says, "go visit my tailor. Bespoke Henry's in Marda Loop. I mean it about your image; you're a walking disaster. At least Gerste put in *some* effort, even if he had shitty taste."

"Once this business is taken care of, I promise."

"Ha! You are such a liar." He checks his watch. "It's been a slice, but I need to jet."

"Me too, I'm on the clock." I look over the thrashed room. "Any chance you can deal with this?"

Galan makes a call. "Clean up on isle six." Gives me a fist bump. "My guy will erase everything, part of my new, full-service plan. Tell your friends."

"Thanks. Consider your debt paid in full."

"Not even close." And he's gone.

A relief, all things considered. I root around and locate my keys, phone, a small stash of cash, and a shiny Slate Resources visitor's pass, the kind you're supposed to return when you exit the building. A plan forms. The *out-of-options-out-of-time-lets-wing-it* kind of plan I specialize in. On goes one of Arnie's pinstripe suits, a wide brimmed fedora, and a splash of his gag inducing aftershave. Tucking my hair under the hat, I don't even recognize myself.

11:02 PM. Cutting it close. The Mustang roars to life and I tear through the dark and pissing rain to a cheap lot three blocks from Slate Tower, a lofty obelisk of black granite and mirrored glass. A geezer gives me the eye from the security desk when I duck through the door.

Dripping hat shading my face, I flash the card and grunt in my best faux-gangster accent. "Hell of a game tonight."

"Fucking Flames fucked it in overtime. Again! Good thing I bet against them." A laugh. "You got another delivery for Mr. Slate?"

I pat a pocket. "Yeah, second part of the package from earlier."

"Go on up then, he's entertaining in his office. Want me to let him know you're coming?"

"Nah, he's expecting me."

"Right then." An elevator dings as it opens. "See you on the flip side."

I get in and relax, relieved and amazed Plan A worked. Plan B would have involved threats and violence and I don't have the energy for either. The top floor, home to Nathaniel Slate's personal suite, is dark and deserted. I stop and curse under my breath. Traditional Chinese lithographs line the walls. Vases, urns, and statues fill shelves and display cases. The bastard is some kind of goddamn Mandarin art collector. I examine each piece but don't see the casket. The clock ticks, trudging closer towards midnight.

A spiral staircase climbs up to a penthouse. I pad up the stairs and find a thick door inlaid with a silver mountain. It's open a crack, leaking a sliver of light, so I slip the Glock from my pocket and creep over. Voices. I recognize Slate's from a recent newscast, stern and clipped, in an old English sort of way.

"I'll help you deal with Umbra once this current business is concluded. Those *scientists* have twice interfered with my own plans."

"Don't underestimate them. They have hidden resources." Another man, one with a strong East Asian accent.

"So do I."

"I appreciate your offer. I do. But I shouldn't require your assistance. In a few minutes, my power will exceed the—"

I feel a presence behind me and spin. A darting shadow. A flash of silver. The gun goes flying and a foot connects with the side of my head, smashing me through the door and onto the floor. The brightness of the room is blinding and I hear Slate yell "don't get blood on my carpet," before the foot connects again.

❖❖❖

Consciousness hurts. I blink away double vision and fight past a raging headache, paralyzed, panicking until I realize my hands and feet are taped to a chair. Nathaniel Slate sits across from me, behind an expansive ebony-topped desk, mouth set in a hard line.

"So, the legendary Tagger Boone, is it?" He says, talking to someone behind me. "Doesn't seem so legendary at the moment."

A young Japanese lady with crimson lipstick, square cut blue-black hair, and skin-tight ballistic nylon walks over and sits on the edge of the desk. "I don't know boss, Gerste and the twins said they put a clip of widow-makers through his heart." I recognize her. Lady Chiyome, executive bodyguard and sword-for-hire. We'd met last year at an industry mixer on Pump Hill. Galan, ever the charmer, had fallen in lust for the night. "He's like a bad penny." She pokes me in the chest with her katana. Frowns.

Slate rubs his chin and leans back. "Mr. Boone. You are alive for one reason. One. My business associate wishes to ask you a question. You will answer that question." From a side room lumbers an enormous, hulking man-shaped creature with tattooed alabaster skin, long wild hair, and a red silk loincloth. "Ping Ji, as you can see, is a Yao Guai, a demonic celestial from the lowest level of Chinese hell. I'd answer his question quickly and truthfully. He's not known for patience."

The demon stops in front of me, bending over until we see eye to eye. The scent is overpowering, thick with dust, snakes, and forgotten crypts. He sniffs, speaks. "Lien Hua."

Flowers. Rain. Memories of a kiss. The princess's imparted strength warms my skin, surrounds me with an aura of invincibility, and washes away the haze fogging my mind.

Lady Chiyome puts her blade to my throat. "Answer the question or die."

I smile, knowing I'm not getting out of here alive, knowing it doesn't matter. "That didn't sound like a question."

With an angry growl, the demon picks up my chair and slams it down hard, cracking the frame. Chiyome slides out of his way, blade caressing my neck. She flicks the blood onto the carpet and gets a nasty look from Slate.

"Lotus Blossom. Where is she?" The demon growls, eyes smoldering.

"Is that the new Chinese buffet down on Seventh Avenue? I haven't been there yet, but I hear the fried chicken is amazing."

He roars and gets back in my face. "I smell her. In your hair. On your skin. She thinks she is clever, that she can thwart my plans, but she is nothing." A clawed hand reaches and stops short. "Fah. It is not worth my time to break her petty wards. In a few minutes, I will be a god and you will burn in endless torment." The Yao Guai pulls back a curtain and opens a French door leading to a shallow balcony. The light of the full moon pierces broken clouds to fall across the room. "Slate! It is time."

Nathaniel Slate watches our exchange with an amused look. "Lady C, if you wouldn't mind." The lithe bodyguard disappears and returns with a simple wicker casket, *the* wicker casket, placing it on the desk and backing away. Rubbing his hands together, Slate flips the small chest open and pulls out a ginseng root. It has arms, legs and a head, and resembles a shriveled doll. "A Greater Root of Power." Holding it to his nose, he inhales and sighs, colour rushing to his face. "Maybe the greatest. Ping Ji, are sure you want to eat this thing?"

"I must devour it at the stroke of midnight, when the full moon weakens the bonds. Only then will the soul within become vulnerable."

"The soul of Wanyan Wu."

"My ancient nemesis. I will gain his power and burn my enemies in the fires of Avīci."

"*Our* enemies."

The demon bares its teeth. "Our enemies."

Slate stands up and tosses a leather-bound tome to Chiyome. Turns back to Ping Ji. "Six minutes. Get ready, she will make the necessary preparations."

The bodyguard pulls my chair and other furniture to one side of the room and draws a circle on the floor with white chalk. She examines the book and adds intersecting triangles and bisecting lines. Eight glyphs. It's a focusing circle, one I've seen before but can't quite place. The chalk glows, kissed by the moonlight.

Three minutes.

When Slate ducks down to retrieve something out of a lower desk drawer, I make my move. Muscles flex and the wooden chair creaks, its integrity ruined when the demon slammed it down. I throw my weight forward and surge up, yanking my arms and twisting my legs, tearing it apart. With various sized pieces still taped on, I scoop up the root and charge out onto the balcony. The city stretches below me, dark and quiet.

Slate's head snaps up. "Chiyome! Stop him."

"With pleasure."

I climb onto a chair, turn around, and teeter at the railing. The princess said I'd need to free Master Wu, release him from his prison. Do I eat the root like the demon was going to? Destroy it? Maybe I'll take a bite on the way down and see what happens. I step back and prepare to high dive, but my legs don't respond. A faint whisper brushes my mind. Lien Hua.

"Wait."

An invisible force holds me in place, the cozy protection spell morphing to bind my lower body. What the hell? Lady C is three steps away so I hold the root up like a shield. "Stop, or—"

"Or what?" She dances in and slices through my outstretched arm at the wrist. Damn, didn't see that coming. The ginseng man falls but I'm quick enough to snatch it out of the air with my remaining hand, watching blood spurt onto the concrete.

A spear of crackling fire blocks a decapitating strike. "Worthless female. You must not damage the root!" Ping Ji hooks her and pulls her back into the office, lifting her in one motion and flinging her against the nearest wall. She falls, stunned, pictures and priceless artefacts crashing around her.

"One minute." Slate, calm again, calls from inside.

The Yao Guai holds up a clawed hand and says a word. Semi-translucent lotus petals appear, twisting around me in the moonlight before the demon digs in his nails and tears them away. Pain rushes in.

"You," he roars, "the root. Now!"

Lien Hua again, reaching into my mind. *"Wait."*

Not that I have a choice, but wait for what? The big smelly demon to rip my head off? To bleed out before he rips me to pieces?

Chiyome charges, pissed off and intent on skewering the demon, but Ping Ji, sensing her intent, steps nimbly to the side. I watch the blade slide along his ribs, watch it impale my remaining hand and the root, feel it penetrate my heart.

"Free." A different voice. Older. Deeper.

Light bursts from the ginseng, coalescing into a withered old man in elaborate phoenix robes. Master Wu? Must be. The sorcerer tips his head before dissipating in a wild display of pyrotechnics.

I take one last glimpse of the room. Stoic Nathaniel Slate leaning against his desk. An enraged Ping Ji sheathed in flame. Lady Chiyome, reeling away. I topple backwards and fall forty-two stories to the street below.

❖❖❖

The car I cannonballed is totaled; the roof cratered and alarm blaring. It's a cherry red Dodge Charger, pure muscle trash, and I sit on the hood struggling to keep from slipping over the edge. Close to oblivion. Real close this time.

There's a lot of blood and Chiyome's unbroken sword transfixes my chest, the carved ivory handle thrusting up like a tombstone. I need to get out here before she comes looking for it. Out of sight. Out of the city. Out of the country. Make that trip to Barcelona like Galan suggested.

Sirens echo in the distance and I will the Guild get here faster. It would only be minutes before the authorities show up and it's damn near impossible to spin a dive like this as a *near death experience*.

I don't wait long. The Jaguar rolls up and a priestess gets to work inspecting my mashed, mangled, and impaled corpse. I get the eye straight off.

"Yeah, yeah, don't give me that shit. It's not like I plan these things."

She searches for something around the crushed mid-life crisis vehicle.

"My arm? I left it upstairs. Way up. Penthouse suite."

With an exaggerated shrug, and a soundless sigh, she fades from sight. Fire flashes forty-two stories up. Ping Ji is still in the game. Still pissed. Oh well, not my problem anymore.

Another spirit materializes next to me, the old man from the root. He takes a deep bow. "I am in your debt."

I return the bow the best a phantasmal puddle can. "My pleasure." Though I'm not sure it is. I have the feeling I've been played, that I'm missing something important.

"How did you come to be there, in the end, at the perfect moment?"

"A descendant of yours, an esteemed lady named Lien Hua."

He raises a bushy white eyebrow.

"A princess, they call her the Lotus Blossom."

"They would." His forehead furrows, gaze distant. "So, the line of the Black Lotus still lives, still meddles. What year is this, in the western calendar?"

"2015." I think about the princess, warm thoughts fading into doubt, into anger.

The old man gives me a concerned look. "You sacrificed your life for mine, gave up your future. What did she offer you?"

Not enough. Sacrificed? No, I would have sacrificed myself. What she did, I realize now, was murder, pure and simple. Okay, maybe not that simple, but I know there'll be a reckoning when I track her down, a dead reckoning.

The priestess reappears clutching my arm. She brushes off patches of rippling flame, sees Master Wu, and stops dead. Energy crackles. Raw power permeates the ether, condensing to wrap the old man in a pulsing bubble. Master Wu rubs his hands and smiles. "Ah, such petulance from youth. How

I've missed it." He bows to me. "We'll meet again." Vanishes in a puff of smoke.

The priestess stands still for a long moment, gives me the eye again, and pulls out the ledger, spinning it at me like she wants to take my ghostly head off. I press my thumb to the print and the counter hits zero. Zero. The finality hammers me. If I die now, before earning another free pass, that would be... the end. I'm not sure how I feel about it. I've always had that golden ticket waiting when I inevitably fuck up.

Snatching the book from my hands, the priestess opens her box of tricks and takes out a flute, a small cloth bag leaking silver dust, and a roll of duct tape.

"All out of bark flayed from the world's oldest tree? Don't answer. Anyways, while you're in there, could you please fix my back? Pretty please? I'll make it worth your while."

The acolyte ignores me and uses the tape to reattach my arm. She sprinkles the dust along each limb and over my pancaked skull. Plays a new song. High pitched. Penetrating. The resulting golden cloud is expansive, surrounding and infusing my entire body in a cocoon of blazing light and pulsing fire.

The wall, this time, is damn near impenetrable. I hit it hard and bounce back. I hit it again. And again. Each time making a small dent, a crack, a hole. The wall fractures and I break though, feeling the patter of rain on my face and smelling the inviting aroma of late night street sausage. Alive. Again.

1

Heart and Soul

Sarah saw the soul wedged in the sidewalk crack and vaulted it with a dignified elegance universally reserved for marathon runners twenty-five miles into a race. Which is to say, she struggled to drag her feet a half inch off the ground, clipped a patch of uneven concrete, and caught herself on a weathered aluminum street sign where a handmade poster bearing a distinctive, stoic face stared down at her. *I'd rather be Walken.* No shit.

The soul fluttered, stirred by an invisible breeze, and let out a weak mew. Damn. Who did these lost spirits think she was? Pasithea? Vivian Darkbloom? She sighed, did a painful U-turn, and strode back to the shabby thing most would have mistaken for a torn plastic shopping bag or a lost race bib. Resting her hands on her tightening thighs, she prodded the soul with the toe of her scuffed Asics. It cozied up and nibbled a shoelace.

"You okay?" The rough voice made her jump. Sort of. Her feet were too tired to leave the ground but the urge was there, resulting in a startled lurch. Another runner? Unlikely. She hadn't seen anyone in ages.

"I said, are you okay?" A zombified old man with patchy hair and a weary gray expression trotted up. He had a purple t-shirt adorned with *I thought they said Rum* and a crumpled number 1999 pinned to unfashionable black shorts.

"I'm not finished yet, if that's what you're asking." Close, maybe, but not quite. Her mind and body teetered on the brink and she knew what this had to be. A doubt. A fear. They'd told her at the start she couldn't outrun her demons.

He held up his hands and regarded her with a disappointed air. "Sorry, you looked a little wobbly."

The soul chose that moment to let out a whimper, a pitiful sob that pulled on her heartstrings and invoked memories of babies, or maybe kittens. It didn't like the man either.

Mister 1999 heard the cry and spotted the ethereal fragment. "Nice, just the snack to get me across the line." He pulled out a water bottle, unscrewed the lid, and bent to scoop it up.

"STOP." Sarah stepped forward to block him. "This one's mine." She didn't want to care, she really didn't, but damn... kittens.

"Come on, at least give me a bite, I'm starving. This race is a nightmare. I know they said there were no aid stations, that it was fend for yourself, but this is ridiculous."

"Well it is the Purgatory Marathon, what did you expect?"

"Something. Anything. Be a darling and share."

"No, I don't think so, now *please* fuck off." It never hurt to be polite. Well, almost never. She could already see where this conversation was heading, but old habits die hard.

The gray man let his shoulders drop, stretched his fingers, and clenched his fists before shoving hard enough to toss her into the air towards the street. She'd always believed her personal demons would be clever, subtle, but this one lacked imagination, all impatience and brute force. Snagging the street sign, she spun like a seasoned pole dancer and dropped to the ground, thrashed legs absorbing the impact and body positioned for the inevitable follow on.

"Fancy." He surprised her by jamming the soul into his bottle and taking off like a bat out of hell. "You can't save them all little girl, you can't even save yourself." A speedy bastard, but it didn't matter. She snapped the sign post off at the base and hurled it, Walken and all, piercing the sprinting vulture's chest and flinging him to the concrete where he flailed, cursing, in an expanding pool of reeking sweat and infernal slime. She walked over and plucked the bottle from his belt, opened it, and added the spirit to the overflowing pouch on her hip. The others welcomed it with enthusiasm. Yes, she'd been right, another damn kitten.

A muted cheer ahead and around the corner, a finisher. 1999 coughed, black blood flowing from his mouth. "You can't win this race, the last mile is the longest mile, the hardest mile. Give up, walk, take the easy road to Hell."

Sarah pondered the last bend in the road, listening to the roar of Paradise. Her demon was right, the last mile sucked, and what could she expect when she finally crossed the line? A halo? Infinite boredom? This wasn't about winning, it was about freedom. For her, for all lost, abandoned souls. She turned, took an unmarked path, and started running.

8

Strength

Sir Meredith took the heavy blow on his shield and spun away, arm numb. Before he could right himself, the giant swung the tree trunk again, catching him in the side, shattering ribs, and tossing him face first into a scum covered pond. He spit blood, then struggled to his feet. "Never," he whispered through clenched teeth. "Never give up." Forcing away the pain, he staggered towards the towering creature and raised his sword to the sky.

"By the Light of Silver Sun and in the name of the King, be gone foul creature, back to the pit you crawled out of."

Madoc, the Giant of Candlewood, rested the oak on his shoulder and laughed, a deep guttural bark that made the young knight's skin crawl. "Your king has no power here, boy, and as you can clearly see, the light is fading. Soon, the entire land will be cloaked in darkness. My darkness."

"Not while I yet draw breath." Sir Meredith reached deep and surged forward to slice through the giant's knee, producing a spray of hot, black ichor. It washed over him. Penetrating. Burning. Madoc's club whistled down again and the knight raised his mangled arm and shield. The blow, the hardest yet, rent what remained of both, driving Sir Meredith's feet deep into the peat. Pain spiked through him, but he swung his sword again, watching it shatter on the oak, bright shards of star laced steel spinning into the gloom. The giant grabbed the knight's arm and lifted him until they were face to face. Eyes of fire seared his soul.

"You are strong Meredith, son of Elidir, the strongest I've faced, but none may draw my blood and live."

Never give up. The knight struggled but he was spent. Broken. Madoc dropped him to the ground, already forgotten, and limped into the gloom.

Sir Meredith lay where he'd fallen, pain replaced by a strange lethargy. Poisoned blood seeped into his body, into bones, and shadows settled into his mind. Calling him. Welcoming him. "It wasn't supposed to end like this," he thought, "I'm too strong."

❖❖❖

Ash and Oak, Peat and smoke,
Silver streams, Forest dreams.

"Did it work?" A whisper above him, a gentle female voice laced with concern and doubt.

"Of course, it worked sister, are you suggesting I miscast the ritual?" Another voice, pair to the first but deeper.

"No, no, it's just..."

"What then?"

"Substituting Golden Samphire for Watercress is risky, the results unpredictable."

"Hush, it will be fine. An unusual substitution, but these things are never exact, too many uncertainties."

"But look at him, he's half the size he was."

The knight didn't understand the conversation. Was he dead? Was this heaven? It didn't seem like heaven. He couldn't see. Couldn't move. He strained to lift his arm.

"Did you see that?"

"A good sign. Get the knife. The sharp one with the stag horn handle."

Sir Meredith felt hands upon him. Heard cutting. Whatever restrained him fell away and soft hands touched his head.

"Careful now, Ash. Careful."

A dim light pushed the darkness away and he stared into the violet eyes of two elfin-faced girls.

"How do you feel?" they said in unison.

To tell the truth, he felt rested. Strong. "Good," he said, his voice sounding odd. Higher and smoother. "I feel good."

They helped him sit up and he took in his surroundings. A tiny cottage with curved wooden walls and round windows. Steps up to a loft. A table covered in books, boxes, and pots. It reminded him of a wizard's study. Where was he? He'd ridden from Perdun on a quest. A dark forest? A terrible giant? Fragments of memory swirled through his mind. Slid away.

The girls saw his frown.

"You have nothing to fear sir knight, we are healers and you are in a safe place. The safest you will find in these dark times."

He relaxed and looked at his hands. Thin, pale, and tiny compared to his oversized paws. Woman hands.

"What is this?" He held one up, turning it, noted the lack of scars, the lack of callouses. Not his hand. "What is this witchery?"

"It was the only way," said the first.

"Let us explain," said the second.

He tried to stand but they held him fast. How? They were but slips of things.

"Madoc's curse is terrible. We found you in the bog, tried to heal you, tried to remove the curse, but you were too far gone."

"So, we used an old magic, one long forgotten, to remove you *from* the curse."

"Madoc? My hands... they are... what have you done to my hands?"

"The giant's blood is cursed to kill any man it touches. Any *man*." The girls handed him a mirror.

He held it up and the reflection of a fair-haired, gray-eyed woman stared back at him.

"It was the only way."

Stunned. Sir Meredith let the mirror drop and slumped across the bed, back into unconsciousness.

❖❖❖

The smell of ginger stirred the knight awake. His stomach growled. How long since he'd eaten? Felt like forever. He swung his legs over the side of the bed and caught another glimpse of his hands. It wasn't right. It had to be a trick. One of the girls placed a wooden bowl onto his lap, a delicious smelling vegetable stew.

"Soon, the entire land will be cloaked in darkness. My darkness."

"My name is Ashley." She pointed to the other. "And that's my sister Silvia. We're faeries, tree spirits, not witches, in case you were wondering."

He stopped shoveling food in his mouth, finished chewing, and swallowed. A life of chivalry and he'd forgotten his manners. Inexcusable. He stood up and bowed. "Sir Meredith, at your service." His voice rang strange in his head, familiar yet not.

"You appear in better spirits today," Sir Meredith," said Ashley with a smile.

"Please call me Merry."

"As you wish Sir Merry."

"Just..." it didn't matter. "Thank you for everything, I don't mean to be ungrateful. It's just..." Just? He didn't know what to say, what to think. "This stew could revive the dead, thank you."

Ashley refilled his bowl. "It's the pepper. Gives it a bite. Hard to find with the merchants avoiding the trade road, but we manage. Madoc chokes the forest in shadow and fear."

Madoc. Memories flooded back with a chilling sense of dread. Riding into the dark forest. His horse bolting. The giant. Falling. Failing.

Merry sagged and curled up on the bed, no longer hungry.

Failed.

The King had trusted in him to defeat Madoc and he'd failed. Failed the Order. Failed the Kingdom. Failed the King.

"You should have let me die."

Ashley took his hand. "We are stewards of the forest. We care for it and for all life. We couldn't let you die."

He pulled away.

"The King gave me this task. Me. Of all his knights, he sought me out to destroy Madoc, just as my father once dealt with the Serpent of Imil-Idr. Only my arm, my strength could prevail."

Silvia laughed.

He glared at her. "You think I jest?"

The fairy looked at her sister who shook her head.

"Tell me. Please."

"You weren't the first knight your king sent to kill the giant."

The words speared his heart.

"Three brave knights in silver mail, fox face shields, and glittering swords rode into the forest a fortnight before you. They fought heroically, bravely, but in the end, they fell in the same bog. We tried to save them but the curse had already devoured their bodies."

Three knights of the fox. The Brother's Rhwyth. They had ridden from Perdun in the dead of night on a mission of urgency, sent into the wild to deal with a dire, though unnamed threat.

Ashley pushed the bowl of stew back into his hands. "Your king had great faith in you if he thought you could prevail where three could not."

"But I... I still failed." Merry held his spoon tight. "The giant lives."

Her hand touched his. "A worry for another day. Eat. Regain your strength. You are welcome to stay with us as long as you want. We will teach you what you'll need to know."

"Teach me?"

"You're a woman now, like it or not. There's a lot to learn."

❖❖❖

Merry twisted braided hair between his fingers. Strange. He'd always had long hair, a fashion of nobility, but he'd worn it straight, with a simple part in the middle. The faeries had taught him much over the past days, so much his mind spun. He didn't like their witchery, didn't like being a woman. Being tiny. Frail. Weak. He'd taken a knife, rested it against his narrow wrist, intent on taking his life. He didn't. He couldn't. The codes of his Order forbid it, suicide assuring eternal damnation.

The girls pored through a thick tome of colourful pictures, arguing with each other. They reminded him of his little sisters, sisters he might never see again. That made him sad, and a little angry. There must be something they could do.

"Why don't you use your witchery... magic to fight Madoc?"

"He's much too powerful. If not for our charms, he would find and eat us. Do you see the candles?" Silvia pointed to beeswax blobs flickering around the room. "They keep our home invisible to him and his many servants. Once the candle light is gone..." Ashley lowered her eyes. "We are bound to this tree. We can leave for a time, but must always return. Madoc knows this."

More magic he didn't understand. "Have you found a way to change me back yet?"

Silvia snapped the tome shut and pushed it away. "The curse will hold as long as the giant lives, perhaps longer. The lore is uncertain. I doubt even the King's pet wizard can break a blood spell this powerful. You might want to speak with him, if anyone knows a way, he will."

"I can't go back like this. I'd be... disgraced." Laughed at. Expelled. The Order of the Silver Sun was an order of men, warriors. They protected women, the foundation of their Code, but they weren't women. The Order wouldn't know what to do. They would send him home where his father would understand even less. No, he couldn't go back. "How long will your candles last?"

"Months," said Ashley.

"Weeks," said Silvia. "The harder he searches for us, the closer he gets, the faster they burn. Will the king send more knights?"

"I don't know." Merry didn't know whom the King *could* send. Shadows rose across the land and the Order responded to each threat with force, losing knights faster than they could be recruited. "I wish I had the strength to defeat him."

Ashley sat beside Merry and took his hand. Squeezed it. "Because you're a woman? You think that makes you weak? Do you think we're weak?"

"No, but—"

She cut him off. "You are still Sir Meredith, Knight of the Order of the Silver Sun, the Bear of Perdun, wielder of the famed blade Ewindal, are you not?"

He was, had been, but now?

"And your heart is strong." She squeezed his hand till it hurt. "The strongest."

He closed his eyes and remembered who he was. "I need my sword."

Silvia pointed to a trunk next to the door.

His tabard, cleaned of peat and mud, wrapped a bundle of gear. He pulled it apart and grasped the hilt of Ewindal, the broken blade now a foot-long sliver. Held it up. The runes along the fuller caught the candlelight and gleamed, still empowered, still thirsty. The sight warmed his heart, ignited his blood.

❖❖❖

Thunder crashed and lightning flashed. Rain pounded down. Merry pulled at his borrowed cloak, caught on some razor-edged brambles, and heard it rip. "Hellfire," he cursed, slipping sideways and almost falling back into a knee-deep stream, knee-deep at least, to Sir Meredith. With a cough, he stumbled to his feet, spit up dirty water, and felt the gaze of the forest heavy upon him. An owl in the crook of a twisted tree, eyes round and unblinking. A conspiracy of ravens. Wolves. All watching. All judging. You shouldn't be here, they whispered, you're weak, pitiful.

He pressed on, trying his best to silence the doubt, and eventually stumbled across the old north-south trade road. He stopped. Right would take him south, to Perdun, to the Court. Left would take him deeper into the forest, closer to Madoc, closer to redemption. Or death. After a long, tired moment, he turned left.

Light fading, the road, no more than a muddy rutted track, widened, the trees cut back to make room for a collapsing barn. Beyond, a flickering lantern illuminated the front of an inn, moss covered shingles jutting over dark stained timbers. Smoke curled from a brick chimney. The inn's sign, an owl snug in a nest, swung in the wind to bang against a closed window shutter.

Merry knew this place, a pleasant and welcoming way station run by a legendary archer and his daughters. A place to warm up, dry off, and rest before continuing his quest. If anyone had the strength to resist the giant, Harlan Drake would.

He picked his way to the entrance. Knocked. Nothing. What time was it? They shouldn't be closed yet. Couldn't be. He leaned his weary frame against the door and eyed the barn. It might have to do.

The door opened with a creak and he pitched backward, catching himself before his sprawl became a fall. A teen girl in a brown dress looked at him with narrowed eyes, noting his filthy torn cloak and drenched misery. "What do you want?"

Abrupt and cold, not the welcome he'd expected. "This is an Inn, last I knew. I need out of the rain and a fire to warm up. Dinner."

"Sorry, we're closed." The girl pushed him back and tried to close the door.

"I've travelled far today. I can pay, if that is your concern." Merry pulled back his hood. "Let me talk to Harlan."

The girl bit her lip, bent her head close. "He... You don't understand. This isn't a place you want to be." She looked out into the storm. "Where's the rest of your party?"

"It's just me."

"Oh bother, I'm going to regret this. Follow and don't say a word till I tell you it's safe."

Pulling Merry inside, the girl barred the door and hurried up a steep set of stairs, down a long hall, and into a small, comfortable room.

"You should be safe enough here, for a time. My name is Evelyn. I wish I could offer you true hospitality, but a shadow has fallen upon this house."

"The giant? Mado—"

Evelyn slid a finger to her lips. "Shush! Don't say his name."

"But..."

"A servant of the evil one has taken residence here. He's a terrible man, an angry creature with sharp hearing."

"Why would your father allow that?" Harlan Drake was a hero of many battles. A legend.

The girl trembled and looked away. "When the giant came, my father took my mother and older sisters and set out to destroy him. They never came back. Just Unwin and his men." She touched her face. "Animals. They told me Ma... the giant had killed my family, that he'd kill me too if I didn't serve them. So now Unwin uses the Nest to keep an eye on the road. He signals the giant when travelers are abroad."

"I do indeed." The door burst in and a hatchet-faced man in a black leather jerkin stomped into the room. "I'd wondered where you'd gotten off to, girl, and now I see you've found a friend." He leered at Merry, sizing him up. "And a pretty lass she is. The boys will enjoy her charms, no doubt, now come along and start dinner. I'm starving."

Evelyn spun, putting herself in front of Merry. "No, leave her be."

Unwin grabbed the girl's arm and flung her into the hallway, shoving her hard against the opposite wall. "You forget your place little Evie."

He pulled a club from his belt. "I think you need another lesson."

Anger flared, driving away Merry's fatigue. Without conscious thought, he stepped forward. "Put down your weapon and leave this place forever. I won't ask again." He stood tall, projecting confidence and authority. A knight's authority.

The man raised his eyebrows. Laughed. "A spirited one. Excellent." He feigned a swing at Evelyn but turned, ramming his club into Merry's stomach. To Merry, the blow seemed slow, awkward, an attack his mind could easily sidestep. His body, however, didn't respond as quickly. He folded, falling back against the bed, heaving, fumbling for Ewindal as the club came down on his arm. The sword clattered to the floor. Unwin saw the broken blade, saw the runes. His scowl became a smile.

"What's this?" The ruffian reached down to pick it up. "A treasure gleaned from the killing fields? Perhaps I should test its efficacy on you."

Crack. The man stopped, teetered. *Crack*. Evelyn swung the chair again, smashing it against the back his head, knocking him to the floor. "You're dead," he croaked, pushing himself up on one arm. "You're both dead."

"No!" Evelyn kicked him in the groin. When he curled up, she kicked him in the head until he stopped twitching. "Never again." She put down the chair and sat on it, burying her face in her hands. "Now I've done it." She began to shake.

Taking a deep, painful breath, Merry bent down and retrieved his sword, bruised arm protesting. He couldn't believe it, saved by a girl, a small, weak girl. He studied her, considered the dead man on the floor. No, not weak, not at all. "You did what you had to."

"I... I know. But when his men find out he's dead, they'll be furious, they'll ra... kill us."

"Then they better not find out."

Evelyn sniffled and wiped her nose with the back of her hand, gave him a questioning look.

"We'll have to catch them off guard, one by one, when they're not expecting it." Expectations. Routines. A plan took shape in his head, a crazy plan, but like Evelyn, he had to do what he had to do.

"Do you know how Unwin warned the giant that travelers were on the road?"

A nod. "He threw a handful of black dust onto the fire. There's a jar of it in his room."

"Simple. Good. So, tell me, how do you feel about revenge?"

❖❖❖

Fading Light, Endless Night
Voiceless Lies, Shadows Rise

A dark form burst from the bubbling mud, massive and hulking, surrounded by fell mist and twisting shadows. Madoc. With a grunt, the giant wrenched a drowned oak from the peat and stripped decaying branches, fashioning a knight-killing club of wicked proportions. He swung it back and forth, testing its balance.

Swaying and shivering, Merry clung to a high branch of a nearby tree, thankful his slight frame blended into the broad leaves. He wanted to leap down, confront the demon head on, but he'd learned that lesson. Stealth and subtly, he told himself. Patience.

Madoc sniffed the air, squinting in Merry's direction, and stomped over to the wall of trees bordering the trade road. Stopping below the knight, the giant grew still. Quiet. A game played many times. Travelers, knights, whomever, ambushed from the shadows and never seen again.

Faint noise in the distance. A jingle. Notes of a song. Evelyn performing her part. The giant pushed his head through the foliage and peered down the road, trying to spy his next victims. He rumbled under his breath and pushed deeper.

Now or Never. Heart beating hard enough to burst, Merry let go of the branch, holding the fragment of Ewindal in both hands, and dropped to spear the giant's neck. Even broken the sword could pierce the monster's demonic hide. His plan, his entire plan hinged on this moment, this instant of surprise.

Time slowed.

Madoc laughed, twisted, and snatched him from the air. The giant's hand, half as big as Merry's body, pinned the knight's arms, holding him tight.

"Aha!" The giant laughed. "What do we have here? A tiny assassin hiding in my shadows?"

Merry, silent, struggled and strained, not giving up.

"Feisty." Madoc held the knight to his face and sniffed again, crimson eyes distant. "You smell familiar. Almost like... No, impossible. You're just a woman, a distraction while more of those accursed knights assail me." The giant squeezed, driving the air from the Merry's lungs, driving life from his body.

Darkness clouding his mind and knowing he had but moments, Merry twisted Ewindal's hilt so that the broken blade turned towards the giant's fingers. The edge cut deep, deeper as Madoc tightened his grip. Light flared. With a howl, the giant flung the knight away and growled, anger and black ichor bubbling out. "I know that blade and you, knight. A trick of the fae, I thought I smelled their reek on you. I'll deal with them after I've crushed your bones and burned away your wretched soul.

Merry landed hard in a slime covered pool, the hilt of Ewindal disappearing into the dank water. He sucked in a deep breath, felt broken ribs grind, and scrambled backwards as the giant raised his club.

"Now die and stay dead this time."

Thock. An arrow plunked into Madoc's temple and stuck there, quivering. It didn't pierce the thick scales, but the giant, distracted, turned to see where it came from. A second arrow, fired from the trees along the road, glanced off his cheek. More followed, striking hand and arm raised in defense. The giant growled, "Rah, so many annoyances." He strode towards the road and stopped, puzzled. Strained to take another step as mud flowed over his feet and lower legs, hardening, trapping.

Arrows? Evelyn? He'd told the girl to make noise and hide, not come blazing in. Hellfire. What else could go wrong? The knight felt a hand on his shoulder and a small, hard object pressed into his hand. Quiet, familiar voices whispered in his ear. "Our spell won't hold long. Eat this, it will help." Ignoring the possible witchery, he popped the root into his mouth, tasting bitterness. Within moments heat surged through him, masking the pain. "I thought you couldn't help, wouldn't help?"

Ashley and Silvia, nearly invisible in green and brown cloaks, pulled out willow switches and began drawing shapes in the air. Wisps rose from bog, swarming the giant, nibbling at the darkness cloaking him. "You never gave up, how could we?"

Roaring as more arrows plunked into him and batting away the wisps, Madoc struggled to free himself, looking back towards Merry and beyond, to the sisters. "Ha! The fae comes to me. They shall make a fine meal." He wrenched both legs free and raised the tree trunk to the sky. "Finis omnium." Black winds swirled, dispersing the wisps.

The knight heard gasps and quiet cries. Ashley and Silvia lifted into the air, ghostly tendrils wrapping them, draining them. No arrows flew and he knew Evelyn, too, must be caught in the giant's sorcery. Why not him? He felt around in the pool for Ewindal as the giant neared, the air growing darker, thicker. The sword? Where had it fallen? He needed its light, needed its strength, or all was lost.

A scream. Ashley? Silvia? He couldn't tell. His hand came upon the hilt of a weapon. Not Ewindal, one unfamiliar, shorter and narrower. Still, though, a sword. With a silent prayer of thanks, he pulled it free and flicked mud away. Saw the fox head on the pommel, the name etched on the cross guard. Cannuill. The Sword of the Sons of Rhwyth. He said the name and the weapon sparked to life, glimmering runes filling him with new hope, a new plan.

Noticing the mottled green glow through the dense gloom, Madoc stopped feeding and leaned on his tree trunk to see what it was. Merry kept the blade out of direct sight. Cowered. "I yield, great Madoc, we yield. Spare us!"

The giant bent further, laughed. "You have a light, one that pierces even my darkness. Give it to me and I may kill you fast and painlessly."

"Yes, of course, here it is."

When the giant's face loomed close, breath like brimstone fouling the air, Merry turned and drove the sword into a crimson eye. It slid in, without effort, to the hilt.

Madoc reared back and screamed, pawing at his face, an explosion of radiance bursting across the meadow. "I am undone!" The giant screamed again and tore the sword free, his cloak of shadows burning away, his sorcerous darkness dispersing. He choked out a pleading "Lady. Save me..." before the bog slurped, sucking him down.

Evelyn crawled from the trees, bow still in hand, and fell to her knees as Ashley and Silvia staggered over, pale but smiling.

The knight felt the fog of war slide away. He'd done it. They'd done it. The monster was dead. Excited, he held up his hands. Thin. Dirty. Woman hands. "I... the curse..."

Silvia helped Evelyn to her feet, gave her a root to chew on. "I said the lore was uncertain. Rejoice, you have slain a great evil and driven the shadow from Candlewood. A heroic victory, one minstrels will write songs about, one storytellers will spin stories of."

Merry turned away. He didn't know what to think. He wanted to be angry, wanted to tell them how they'd ruined him, how they'd stolen his strength, but he'd killed a giant, a *giant*, with these hands.

Ashley picked up the fallen sword, held it out. "Stay with us. Defend the forest. There are other evils, other perils here. Evelyn needs your strength. We need your strength. The forest needs your strength." She curtsied. "We would be proud to have you, Sir Meredith."

"Merry," he said. "Just Merry."

The knight held up the sword with strong hands and watched the sun burn away the shadow.

9

Secret Hate

The Devil stood over the twin bed and watched the boy sleep, noting with distaste the floral patterned curtains and deep shag carpet. The seventies. He hated this decade. It reminded him of an overexposed Polaroid picture: grainy, out of focus, and inundated with tarnished gold and repulsive brown. It assaulted his sense of style, one honed by millennia in fire and shadow and perfected by Brioni and Berluti. He didn't want to be here, didn't want to mess around in past, but the eternal conflict needed a nudge, and by god, he was going to give it a shove.

Smoothing the front of his silk jacket, a narrow package marring the perfect lines, The Devil called out the boy's name.

"Max."

A strong name, from old Roman times, it slithered around the room, bouncing from toy to toy, before toppling the house of cards swaying above a book-strewn table. Without waking, and with a faint sigh, the boy rolled into the soft glow of the winter moon, angelic face poking through a mop of long blond hair.

"Max. Wake up." Raising his voice, the Devil prodded the boy's shoulder with a manicured fingernail.

"Santa..." A tornado in flannel pajamas burst from the tangle of blankets, pressing against the windowsill to peer out the frost-etched glass, twitchy elbows knocking aside Matchbox race cars.

The Devil cleared his throat and the boy spun, hands up, stopping when he saw the dark, shifting form, little more than a silhouette. A squint. A head tilt. "You're not Santa."

"No," the Devil whispered, "I'm not."

Max froze, eyes boring deep into the shadows, panic draining away. After a moment, he started to breathe again and turned back to the window.

The Devil dumped a pile of clothes from a wooden chair, reversed it against the bed and sat, leaning his arms across the chair back. "I've heard stories about you Max."

The boy scratched lines through the frost, jagged fingernails trailing a dusting of white.

"Frightening stories."

"You're one of the ghosts from my Christmas Carol book, aren't you?" asked Max, gesturing absently to a shelf bursting with well-worn spines." Are you here to punish me?"

"Do you deserve to be punished?"

A shrug. "I'm terrible and wicked, everyone says so." Max wiped a wet finger on his shirt.

"Who says? Your family? The children at school? The *Church*?"

Another shrug. "Everybody."

"I'm not here to punish you, Max, I'm here to free you."

The boy peeked over his shoulder and tried to pierce the gloom, tried to see the truth. "Are you Death? Father Murphy says the wages of sin is death."

"A steep price," said the Devil, noting the bible on the nightstand, "but not everything in God's book is that simple. Have you ever heard the verse that goes 'A time to love, and a time to hate; a time of war, and a time of peace.'?"

Max shook his head, drawing a tall, narrow tower in the frost, its needle spire stretching towards the heavens.

"No? There are gems buried in that chapter. Diamonds. Tell me, what do you hate the most?"

The boy paused. "I don't hate anything."

"That's not true. I can see it in your heart."

Max bit his lip, drawing a small window at the top of his tower.

"Do you know that everyone has a secret hate, one that smolders deep inside, waiting to ignite? Everyone." Great back wings unfurled from the Devil's back, filling the room and blotting out the moonlight. Twists of shadow-stuff encircled the boy, lifting him above the bed, binding him, snuffing out a cry. "Your secret hate is special Max, unique maybe. It's time to let it out, time to let it burn."

The boy strained against the bonds, twisting and turning. "Let me go."

"I can't," said the Devil, smacking his hand on the chair back, "to much depends on it." He reached into the boy's mind, rummaging through memories and emotions until he found the sea of nightmare. The endless expanse looked placid, serene, but madness lurked below the surface. "The only good is knowledge and the only evil is ignorance." The Devil stopped, realizing that quoting Socrates strayed into the philosophical, the naked concepts of good and evil, of light and darkness, of logic and reason, didn't mean anything to the child. Not yet.

"I said I wouldn't punish you Max, but this *will* hurt." The Devil tightened his grip and forced Max below the surface. "One day you'll thank me."

❖❖❖

A young boy and his older sister held their breath under an ugly brown sofa, intent on the scene playing out in their living room. Beyond a tinsel covered Christmas tree, five candles clutched in dried, withered hands, flickered, illuminating a hunched figure in red felt and black boots, a grotesque elf with mismatched bat ears and a crooked beak nose. The creature tossed down the ritual plate of cookies, chugged the glass of milk, and groaned, rubbing his distended belly.

Father Christmas, Santa, began stuffing handfuls of candy and tiny wrapped parcels into the row of stockings hanging from the fireplace mantle, stopping when he reached the final one, frowning when he read the name sewn into the cuff. Fishing a notebook from his pocket, the elf thumbed off the elastic binding and leafed through the pages. Stopped. Spit. "I thought I recognized this house–" he muttered under his sour breath, ripping the stocking from its nail and dropping it on the floor, "–and this naughty, naughty... *boy*." Stomping on the fallen sock with a heavy boot, he emptied the rest of the stockings back into his bag, snatched the candles, and disappeared up the chimney in a flash of red and white.

Crawling from the shadow of the sofa, the girl pulled the boy to his feet and shook him. "See! I told you. Now do you believe me?" She pushed her face into his, nose touching nose, green eyes boring into gray. "It's not mom and dad."

The boy pulled himself away, shaking in anger, hands curling into fists.

"I don't know what you did, how you got on his list, but you've ruined Christmas. Again." She stormed up the stairs, kicking bannister spindles until they cracked. "I hate you! We all hate you!"

A long crystal icicle, an ornament relegated to decorative duty, had fallen from the mantle top crowded with ceramic figurines. The icicle's facets reflected the tree lights, its broken tip sharper than any natural sliver of frozen water. Max reached down and picked it up, staring at his sister's vanishing back.

❖❖❖

The Devil pulled Max from the water, letting him catch a metaphysical breath. The boy choked and hacked, coughing up a lungful of nightmare. "Last Christmas didn't work out very well did it Max? And the one before that, the same, right? Santa knows what you are, what you will be." The boy gasped, sucking in air, and tried to tear himself from the Devil's grasp. "You have the opportunity, the rare opportunity mind you, to make sure it never happens again, to you, to anyone. Take it Max." The Devil shoved him back under.

❖❖❖

Max stuffed a stack of books into his locker, grabbed his coat, and flipped the door closed with a clang.

"Hey look, it's the naughty one." An older and much larger boy wearing a jaunty red Santa hat sauntered up, two companions trailing behind. He poked Max's chest. "We heard about Christmas loser, a frickin' tragedy if you weren't such a freak."

"Screw off, Eric." Max pushed past the trio, stumbling when one of them stuck out a foot.

"Big words for a boy who never gets any presents. How does it feel to live in the one house

Santa hates? Your sister told us your parents buy stuff to put under the tree. Is that true?"

"Who cares," said Max, doing a little hop to stay on his feet, and backing against a trophy case hanging on the wall across from the lockers. "Christmas is stupid."

"No. You're stupid," said Eric, "very, very stupid." The two bullyboys grabbed Max and pinned his arms while Eric punched him in the stomach, snorting when Max doubled over. When Eric swung his fist again, Max lifted both legs, kicking out, feet spinning wildly. He got in a couple of good shots before the larger boy backed off, brushed a dusty footprint off his t-shirt, and fingered a tear. "You'll pay for that, dickhead." Eric charged, dropping his shoulder into Max's thrashing feet, smashing him through the plate glass protecting the trophies. Max dropped to the floor, broken glass avalanching over him.

"The cool thing is, we can do stuff like this, beat the living shit out of you, and we still get reindeer on the roof." Eric drove a shoe into Max's side, listening to ribs crack. The other boys laughed and joined in. "Face it, Max. You're on Santa's shit list. You'll always be on Santa's shit list. And you know what? Smug, self-righteous little shits like you deserve it. You think you're smarter than

FISHING WITH THE DEVIL AND OTHER FIENDISH TALES

everyone, better, but you're not. You're just stupid."

Max thrashed with each kick, broken glass grinding, lacerating. One hand guarded his face, but the other curled around a long, narrow shard. He made a fist, blood flowing where it sliced his palm.

❖❖❖

Hate leaked from the boy when the Devil pulled him up again, the nightmare spewing from straining lungs. "The spirit of the season, Max, ruined by Santa and well... everyone. That wasn't the worst of it, though, was it?" The Devil forced him into the water one final time. "If you want to be free, you need to free your hate."

❖❖❖

"Nice to see you again Max," said Roger, the school guidance counsellor. "We haven't had an evening session in some time, have we?" The older man, decked out in a cheap, tight fitting Santa suit, got up from his desk and walked across the room to the door, locking it and pulling the shade across a narrow strip of window.

"I heard about your run in with Eric, you shouldn't provoke him."

"I didn't—"

"Shush. Everyone, from the Principal, to your schoolmates, to your parents, is concerned that if you keep this up, keep picking fights, you're going to end up expelled or in the hospital." He gave Max a hard look. "Are you cursed to make enemies? Cursed to cause trouble wherever you go?"

Max pushed himself deep into the chair and hugged his ribs, feeling the bandages and bruises. It hurt to breath, to talk, so he didn't. Nothing he could say would matter anyways. Instead he glared at the man, teeth clenched, dark thoughts bubbling.

"I can help you Max, like I always do." The councilor unfastened his belt, pulling the wide leather through the buckle, a black snake with brass fangs. Max watched it uncoil and grow, an angry, menacing viper. "Do you like the suit? I heard Santa didn't come to your house again this year so I thought you might like a present."

Despite the pain, Max fought harder than he ever had, screaming, kicking, biting, until the fat man lost patience and flung him across the room, headfirst into a wall. Now dizzy and struggling to breath, the belt tight around his throat, Max pawed at the thick leather with one hand and flailed with the other. The councilor grunted and pushed the boy's head down into some papers, knocking over a mug and scattering pens. A letter opener bumped hard and cold against his cheek. He grabbed it.

❖❖❖

"A time to kill, and a time to heal; a time to break down, and a time to build up."

The Devil watched the boy embrace the truth, or at least, a truth, secret hate burning away fears and nightmares. Empowering him. Freeing him.

"There's only one way to keep your freedom, Max. The Devil reached into his coat and pulled out a thin box of polished ebony. He popped it open, removed a red crystal knife, and placed it in the boy's smoldering hand.

Somewhere a clock struck midnight, as the Devil listened to the sound of hooves on the roof, the tinkle of bells, and the scuffle of boots in the chimney. He patted the boy's shoulder. "His heart. Strike hard, strike fast."

Max held up the knife like a sword, dissecting the moonlight and sending phantom rainbows in every direction. His eyes grew wild, bursting with rage, and his skin erupted in black flame, pajamas burning away in a cloud of hissing cinders. Raw hate infused the air, tinged with death, doom.

Without a backwards glance, the boy slid off the bed and down the hallway, stopping momentarily at two rooms, before floating down the stairs on a river of blood. Max wouldn't stop at the chimney, the Devil knew, wouldn't, couldn't. Another verse whispered across the night. 'For they sow the wind, and they shall reap the whirlwind.' With one hell of a shove, creation trembled.

10

Rust

Captain Alexa Sinclair leaned against the bar, tugged down her combat pants, and pressed the sleek chrome auto-injector against her ass. Just when she had it all worked out, just when the stars aligned for the big score, boom, another fucking disaster. The injector hissed and the chemical cocktail burned its way through her bloodstream, beating back the demon for another day.

"Need a hand Captain?" Bing, the mess hall bartender leaned on his broom, his silver eyes fixed on her anemic skin.

Alexa tugged up her pants and sat, muscles quivering, waiting for the nausea to subside. "Don't worry Bing, if I ever need a sexless, crapped out android for a good time, you'll be the first one I'll call."

"Promises, promises."

"I mean it." She hunched over the bar and grimaced into her cup of coffee. "God, this tastes like shit. Any of that Jaru whiskey left?"

"You told me not to serve you alcohol on weekdays."

"I said what?"

"Last week. You stormed in here screaming about the assholes in Command, the stupid war, and how the air-cooling system in your quarters was down again. Then, after blowing the ceiling full of holes, you tried to kill yourself with that over-proof brandy Fitz brought back from New Arequipa." Bing limped to the window and raised the shutters, letting dawn slide through the slits. Alexa squinted and blocked the light with her hand.

"Doesn't ring a bell. Now, how about that whiskey?"

Bing continued sweeping.

Clunk. A sleek tri-barreled pistol, gleaming with fresh sealant, slammed onto the bar top.

"Dammit Lex, you said you'd shoot my arms off if I gave you any. Make up your bloody mind." The android tossed the broom into the corner and rummaged through a cabinet. A tall purple bottle joined the gun.

Alexa started to pour the rotgut into her cup, changed her mind, and took a long pull instead. Shuddered. She should have stuck with the coffee.

"So," asked Bing, pulling up a seat, "what did the latest diagnostic say?"

A translucent data pane spun his way. "Be my guest."

The android read for a couple of minutes. "A ferrophagic proteobacterium ... aggressive ... terminal ... immediate instauration recommended." He paused after the last phrase. "At least it's not communicable."

"Not between humans," she said, picking at the label on the bottle, "or androids."

"That's a relief. The last thing I need is an incurable, blood-devouring, alien STD. What the hell were you thinking?"

She ignored him. "Looks like I have a week to get a new body, maybe a little more if I keep flooding myself with bootleg pharmaceuticals. That malfunctioning piece-of-shit auto-doc should have identified the exact strain two months ago instead of leading me on with that severe iron-deficiency anemia crap."

Bing nodded. "I'm working on transport to Odysseus. Anything I can do in the meantime?"

"Just keep the drinks coming and scrub the medical records again. If Command finds out, I'll end up an experiment in a Minervan research lab." Alexa put the gun to her head and mimed pulling the trigger.

The door slid open and she straightened as a tall man in shifting camouflage strode in. Sweat beaded on his sun-darkened face and dripped from his close-cropped hair. He saluted. "Ma'am."

"At ease, Zed. Report."

The sergeant wiped his face with his scarf and watched her take a drink, disapproval clouding his face. "A long-range scout identifying itself as the *HMSS Tisiphone* just landed on the upper pad. It came directly from headquarters with no warning. Your presence is requested."

"Save my seat Bing, here we go again." She gave the android a nod, holstered her pistol, and walked out.

"A Major Jonathon Ballard wants to see you," said Zed, matching her long strides and unslinging his short-barreled wire-cutter, "he sounded angry."

She missed a step.

"You know him?" Zed asked.

"Yes." Ten years ago, during the blood bath on Procyon IV, he'd been a glory crazed Lieutenant in her recon company. He'd ended up in pieces; clinging to life in a cylinder of bio-gel, while Command threw her under the bus and exiled her to the ass-end of the galaxy. Old memories, old wounds.

The base's wall loomed to the left, a ridged fortification sheathed in textured defensive plating. She climbed a set of weathered steps and looked across the forested valley stretching into the distance.

Zed joined her, eyes searching the trees below. "And?"

"We served together in the Frontier Expeditionary Taskforce. Fights hard. Plays harder." She kicked a rust-eaten chunk of metal off the barrier. "I heard he went into Special Operations after that fiasco, specialized in covert action, forced diplomacy, that sort of thing. He led the final pacification initiative here on Beta Novos. Knows the lay of the land. The natives. He bring anyone with him?"

"A tactical assault droid. Big one."

"Lovely." Paranoid bastard, this day looked worse every minute.

"Orders?"

"Same as always."

ROBERT BOSE

❖❖❖

Major Ballard. Big, wide shouldered, with jet black skin and shock white hair, sat in her chair reviewing the previous month's operation reports. He looked up and slammed a data pane on the desk. "Five years. It took an entire brigade five years to pacify this god-forsaken planet and somehow you've managed to fuck it up in two."

Alexa stood with her hands behind her back, fingers entwined. If he wanted to play that old game, she could too.

"With all due respect, *sir*, we haven't received the resources required to do squat around here. Two years ago, I had a full company complemented by recon and attack craft. With transfers to line units, chronic attrition, and the bloody environment, I'm down to jack shit." She kept her voice steady and wished she had Zed's stoic composure. The sergeant stood at attention and kept his mouth shut.

"I know this place is hell on equipment and personnel, and I know you've been requesting both, but that's not the issue today."

"That's exactly the issue!"

"No, it's not. Do you think I'd bend all the way from HQ just to give you the gears? I would have sent a harshly worded message." The Major trapped her with a hard stare. "The reason I'm staring at your ugly face right now is the recent destruction of Outpost Gamma. Eighteen casualties, eighteen troopers snuffed out under suspicious circumstances. Your report was short on facts and long on conjecture."

She bristled. "Short on facts, my ass. We have a rogue bug faction calling for civil war. I have to keep an eye on them, regardless of my assets. It's my goddamn job. I can't prove it, but I'm sure Prince Ma'la'mor destroyed the Outpost."

"The crux of the matter." The Major tapped the tablet and brought up a picture of slender, child-sized alien with enormous compound eyes. "Recognize her? Of course you do. Queen W'yn'ea, the leader of the Jaru and your fucking liaison. When you have a problem with dissidents, you deal with her and she makes the problem go away. That's the deal. That's always been the deal. With the war dragging on, resources are being rationed. You're not expected to do anything besides protect the mine, act as a symbol of Colonial power, and keep civil relations with the Matriarchy."

"You forgot about the Church, they—"

"Are not important. I know General Gladstone encourages you to play guardian angel, but they're not a goddamn priority when you're spread thin."

He stood up and loomed over her. "The Queen, however, is. She's a scary little freak and not to be messed with." His eyes narrowed. "Tell me the truth, what the hell did you do to piss her off?"

"Just a small misunderstanding. She said I needed to make amends. Restitution. I've been trying, but she just ignores me."

The Major scrolled to the account in question. "You said she claims you insulted her family, her honour. They're goddamn insects, how did you manage that?"

Blood rushed to her face. She opened her mouth, closed it.

Ballard softened for the first time. "I thought so. You never change, do you L... Captain? Still finding new and novel ways to piss off the locals."

Zed coughed and the spell broke.

"Yes, sir." She relaxed, the energy in the air fading, relieved the opening move of the game was over.

"I'm going to spend the day going over your reports with a fine-tooth comb and interviewing what's left of your command. Then, first thing tomorrow, I'm going to visit the Outpost."

Zed spoke. "I wouldn't advise that sir. The area is still hot."

"No need Sergeant, I have all the support I require. Right M10?"

With a low whine, the tactical assault droid stepped in front of the doorway. It stood two and half meters tall, a hulking humanoid machine sheathed in black matte armour, bristling with weapons. Where the hell had that monstrosity been hiding?

"Proto-type army in a box." Ballard smiled, brilliant teeth giving him the look of a demonic jack-o-lantern. "Told the boys at headquarters I'd give him a field test. Eats bugs for breakfast."

She and Zed exchanged a glance. The deep forest air, laced with bacteria happy to consume non-native metallic compounds, made a mess of mechanicals, chewing them up and spitting out their bones. Ballard should know that.

The Major picked up the tablet, gave the Captain a subtle nod, and went back to reading. "Dismissed."

❖❖❖

Alexa lay on her bed, suffocating. Her head spun. Her heart raced.

"With a low whine, the tactical assault droid stepped in front of the doorway."

She gasped, scrounging for air, but the quick, shallow breaths didn't provide enough. She flailed, spasming arm knocking over a drink, and felt around for the injector she'd left on the night table. Where the hell was it. There. She jammed the textured cylinder against her butt, relaxed, letting her lungs open up. Two shots in one day, or was it three? Maybe it didn't matter, in less than a week she'd have a new body. Someone else's body, sure, but it beat the alternative. She'd go dark; get one with dusky skin, raven black hair, and hazel eyes, the opposite of what she saw in the mirror every day. Did Ballard like black hair?

Ballard. Why him and why now? Was he a threat or an opportunity? Years ago, she could have exploited him, used him to get off this bloody rock, but now? She refilled her glass, and closed her eyes, letting the amber liquid, oak and smoke, carve its way down her throat.

Tap. Tap. Tap. There he was. The vid showed him standing in the shadows of the doorway. No uniform, just flip-flops, shorts, and a crisp white short-sleeved shirt. He glanced around, lips tight, and knocked again.

Tap. Tap. She loosened her robe and opened the door. He frowned at her exposed cleavage. "Captain, please, I'm here on official business."

"Right." She hauled him inside. "Later."

She slid her arms around his neck and kissed him hard. He still had the same smell she remembered, a strong blend of lavender and cedar.

He pushed her away. "You never change, do you?"

She let her robe fall open, pale body glistening in the heat, and slid forward to undo the top button of his shirt.

He grabbed her arm and twisted, the harshness invoking a flood of memories. Good memories. She slipped the hold, hooked her leg behind his, and pushed him onto the floor. He tried to roll, or at least catch himself, but she kicked his arm out from under him and he smacked the floor hard enough to lose his breath. Before he recovered she pounced, straddling his chest and pinning his arms with her knees.

"Old and slow," she taunted.

He grunted and heaved, tossing her against a bank of shelves. "Enough!"

Alexa sulked to her feet and drained her drink. Lieutenant Ballard had been a passionate man of action, whose priorities always involved sex, alcohol, and fighting, in no particular order. Major Ballard had become the kind of man who showed up, late at night, at the room of a half-naked woman, for a bloody conversation.

Well, this was her game now. She smiled and turned up the heat. "Ready for round two?"

"Jesus Christ, harness those hormones for a second and let me talk." He pulled himself to his feet, smoothed down his shirt, and rubbed his back.

"Are you serious?" She slid over to the table and picked up the bottle. "At least have a drink for god's sake."

He shook his head. "I'll get right to the point. What do you know about Blood Lust?"

"The drug? Not much. Why?"

"Someone is smuggling an extra potent variety, prohibited curiosities, and exotic sex slaves off this planet. Command is extra concerned about the drug. It turns people into tireless, super-strong anger management issues before burning out their adrenal glands and who knows what else. I've been tasked with shutting down the smugglers."

"Sounds like a thankless job." Alexa poured two fingers into a glass and pushed it into his hand.

He frowned at her and put it on the table. "It is. So, anything you want to share? The evidence we have points to military connections. That's why the pony show for Sergeant Zed."

She shrugged. "It can't be us, our single transit capable ship got recalled eight months ago. I'd guess pirates. They come and go with impunity these days."

"Pirates?" There was an edge to his voice she didn't like. "That's all you have for me, really?"

"Oh, I have a lot more. Did I mention how miserable and lonely this hellhole can be?" She slid over and wrapped her arms around his neck again. This time he didn't resist. He crushed her to his chest and kissed her hard before pushing her away, a faraway look in his eyes.

"Lex, there's nothing I'd rather be doing, but this isn't the time."

She pouted. "You owe me."

"I do." He traced the long white scar that ran down her face, followed it along her neck and across her breast. "Once I'm done my investigation we can celebrate till we're black and blue." He kissed her again and fled out the door.

❖❖❖

With the twin suns beating down and turning the morning rain into a stifling mist, Ballard puffed on a cigar and leaned against the Wolverine, a combination armoured transport and assault platform. "I'd forgotten how hot it could get." He ran his hand along vehicle's decaying skin and rubbed the grit between his fingers. "And how corrosive. This piece of shit looks ready for the scrap heap."

"That's the best one." Alexa pointed to open hangar behind him, a gaping maw cut into the side of the cliff wall. Mechanicals applied a thick layer of protective lacquer to another weathered war wagon. "Only two of the four we got this year still run. A coat of pretty paint hides a lot of rust around this place."

"No doubt. According to Command, a freighter was dispatched weeks ago with a full load of parts and weapons."

"Never arrived."

"Those goddamn pirates you mentioned? They're getting brazen if they're taking out Colonial transports now. I'm going to recommend a special task force to stomp all over them, like we used to do." Ballard dropped the butt of the cigar, ground it out, and watched M10 climb aboard the Wolverine. "A job for tomorrow though, daylight's burning."

"Last chance to keep your hands clean and join me for a drink and a slow dance. I'm buying." She gave him a rude salute.

"You never quit, do you?"

"I can't, you should remember that."

The Wolverine groaned and pitched before rising off the landing pad and gliding over the base wall. Once the vehicle vanished into the distance, she sagged and held up a trembling hand, cold and blue.

Zed strode up. "We just received a message from Foreman Valentine. She wants you to come down to the mine. Sounded urgent."

"It always is with her."

"Shall I tell her you're on your way?"

Alexa stuffed her hands in her pockets. "Could you handle it? I'm not feeling so hot this morning, going to visit medical."

"Yes ma'am. I'll take care of it."

❖❖❖

Alexa drifted to her office, took her meds, and sent a message to the opposite side of the valley. She should have done this last night but something had stopped her. Sentimentality? Hope? Whatever it was, she couldn't afford to let the past cloud the future. Her life hung by the thinnest of threads.

A young man's face appeared on the screen, brightening when he saw her. "Captain, what a pleasure. What can the Church do for you today?"

"How are you holding out down there, Father? Any trouble?"

Father Ryan stared at her for a second and tucked an errant lock of tangled black hair behind an ear. "Why do you ask?"

"High Command sent an investigator to look into our little operation."

"That is... unfortunate."

"To say the least. It's going to require a divine intervention."

The priest tugged at his collar and patted the sweat off his brow. "How soon?"

"Immediately. He's over at Outpost Gamma right now."

"Won't they just send another?"

"Doubt it. The vein of weapon grade Dicio Crystals is exhausted and this place is too much of a disaster to keep throwing resources at. Once the mine goes, Command will abandon the system and close the transit point."

"Thankfully God's work here is nearly done."

Yeah, if God's work included smuggling drugs, stealing ancient artifacts, and selling bug boys. "Do this, and I'll consider your debt repaid in full."

The priest sighed. "Fine, I'll talk to Ma'la'mor."

"Just offer him the weapons pod we *diverted* a couple of weeks ago and tell him that Ballard, the one from the pacification, is back and on his way to the Outpost. He'll jump all over that. Guaranteed. He still holds a grudge from what I hear."

"The weapons? Are you sure? He's an angry little psychopath, there's no telling what he might do if he gets his hands on those."

"Relax, he hates Ballard a hell of lot more than he dislikes you. Start packing up."

"I'll take your word on that." He didn't have much choice.

"Thanks Father." She ran a hand through her bleached hair, flicking away the strands that came loose, and yawned, oblivion tugging eyelids closed. Images swirled, a young woman with a dark and muscular body, lightning bolts, an alien boy, more beautiful than he had any right to be, a broken man in a bio-gel cylinder. He cracked a jack-o-lantern smile.

❖❖❖

Alexa adjusted her chair for the umpteenth time, leaned back, and put her feet up on the desk. No, still not right. She dug a different calibration tool out of the drawer and plunked herself back onto the floor.

Zed knocked, entered when she barked, and peered over the desk. "Captain?"

"It took me months to get this chair to recline properly and a couple of hours for him to bugger the pneumatics." She stood up and gave it a hard kick. "Fucking piece of shit."

"Ballard or the chair?"

"Yes."

"Want me to find a tech-mech?"

"No, it'll give me something to do while I wait for him to return and remind me about how much of a screw-up I am." She waved the tool at Zed. "What did Valentine want?"

"Nothing special, just who our mysterious visitor was. She wasn't keen to learn Ballard was heading down into the valley. Thinks he'll provoke the natives, says the drums of war are already beating. Same old."

Beep. Beep. The wall screen lit up and indicated a transmission from Father Ryan. The man had aged ten years over the last few hours, his hair matted with sweat and collar askew. Eyes wide and darting to look beyond the screen. He ducked as the thrumming of pulsed weapon fire echoed in the background. "Oro Omo Base? Please answer. This is an emergency."

"Oro Omo, Captain Sinclair speaking."

"Captain? Thank God. We need your help."

"What the hell is going on?" She asked, guessing the answer.

"The Jaru have gone berserk. Something... something happened down river. A battle. They are flooding out of their holes and attacking everything in sight. We could use some assistance. *Zeeeep Boom.* A loud explosion rattled the walls behind the priest.

"That was a proton grenade. Are you sure it's not pirates?" asked Zed. "It fits their MO."

Father Ryan shook his head. "No, it's the Jaru, Ma'la'mor and his clan. You need to hurry. Don't forget I still have the packages. Your pack—"

"I'll have a team there in forty minutes. Hold tight." Alexa cut the channel and turned to Zed. "Take the last Wolverine and burn them all down, those tiny bastards need to learn a hard lesson."

"On it." He stopped and looked at her. "What did he mean about the packages?"

"Whiskey."

"And that's important?" He raised an eyebrow.

She shrugged. "They're a bunch of crazy zealots, happy to risk their lives in the middle of a hostile jungle to bring God to the insect kingdom. What do you expect?"

"Maybe." He looked unconvinced and spun as a different realization struck. "Shit, Ballard is still out there. We better give him a heads up."

"He and his army-in-a-box can take care of themselves. I'm more worried about the Mission. And the mine, we should warn Valentine. And us. Damn, we better bring the perimeter defenses up to full power. We don't want to them to get any ideas."

Zed activated the long-range com. "Major Ballard, please respond." No reply. He tried to connect to the Major's Wolverine. Offline. A ping to the assault droid wasn't returned. He looked at her.

"I could be wrong. Swing by the Outpost on the way and check it out."

"Will do." He spun and double-timed it to the door.

Alexa sent a message to Valentine, put the base on high alert, and walked, slowly, to the officer mess hall. Bing was polishing glasses, like he always did when bored and killing time, oblivious of the wailing alarms.

"Part of the plan?"

"For the most part." She leaned her head against her arms and closed her eyes, tried to relax, failed. "Ballard's out of the picture and the natives are rising up. Good old Ma'la'mor just attacked the mission. Why couldn't that son of a bitch have waited till tomorrow? I've sent Zed out to deal with the situation, but we'll have to leave ASAP, ideally before he gets back."

"I thought that might be case. The cracker program's already breaking the code to Ballard's ship."

"Excellent, what would I do without you." She managed a half-smile.

"Die? Speaking of dying, have you looked in a mirror recently? You look like shit."

"I'm all out of Ferrinephrine. You have anything to take the edge off? Perk me up? I'm falling apart." She felt like an old-time clock, winding down, ever so slowly, every so surely.

The droid pulled out a clear bottle marked with hazard symbols. "I thought you might need a boost, so I mixed you up something special. It'll give you breathing room for a couple of hours."

She poured an entire glass down her throat, pounded the bar top with a fist, and wheezed as fire raged through her system. Her communicator beeped.

"What's your status Sergeant?"

"Bad news at the Outpost. The priest was right, the Jaru are on the warpath, I'm guessing they made a deal with the pirates. Ballard's Wolverine looks like it took a hit from a Brimstone cluster rocket. He put up a good fight though; there must be three hundred dead bugs scattered around. Not just Ma'la'mor's either, lots of royal drones."

The Queen knew which way the wind was blowing. She'd never get a better chance to wipe us off her planet. "And the Major? M10?"

"The droid ate some serious ordinance, parts everywhere. No sign of Ballard. The bodies are three deep in places, though. I'll find him."

"Don't linger, I'm sure he's dead. Anything else?"

"There's a pillar of smoke in the direction of the mission."

"Boot it, the Church is your priority now."

"It's ugly out here, I recommend returning to bolster our defenses."

"Negative, proceed with your mission. That's an order."

A short pause. "Acknowledged. Zed out."

Alexa put her head down again, mind spinning despite the noise and stimulants. She picked at a scab on her arm, one that wouldn't heal despite repeated application of med-patches.

Her com hissed back to life. "... under attack, I repeat, we are under attack by the Jaru. They have heavy weapons, rockets. Nadir, Fitz, and Patty are dead. The Wolverine is coming apart at the seams. I'm not sure we can make it back to base, much less the mission."

She blinked, focused. "Get the hell out of there and come home, the priests aren't worth dying for."

"Yes ma'am."

When the screen went dark, she stood, kicking the corner of the bar, putting dents in the hardwood with the toe of her boot. "Why? Why does this keep happening to me?" She flung her glass across the room.

"We need the packages from the mission," said Bing, moving to sweep up the sparkling fragments. "They're the only items valuable enough to cover the cost of a new body. Unless, of course, you want to trade Ballard's ship."

"The mind swappers won't touch military hardware and we don't have the time to divert to the Black Moon. Odysseus is a five-day trip and who knows what might be lurking around some of those outer rim transit points. We might need detour."

"I don't see any other options."

She tipped the bottle back and let the fire roll through. "I do."

❖❖❖

Ten minutes later Alexa stood in the main hanger, buckling on her powered combat armour amid the bustle of scurrying mechanicals. A battered red unit pushed a helmet into her hands.

"Thanks Suzy."

The obsolete old bot tilted and bobbed its rust pitted face, one step away from falling to pieces, one step away from oblivion. She knew the feeling.

Two more bots dragged her hover bike onto the deck, cleaning off the accumulated grit and dust with a heavy blower. The bike had been in sealed storage for a year, waiting for parts, but that only served to slow the decay, not stop it. She snapped on her helmet and slid into the saddle, the long silver beast shuddering to life with a lopsided, irregular whine. At least it started. She tried to recall why she'd mothballed it. Stabilizers? Lift unit? She increased the power and watched two indicators flicker between orange and red. Ah yes, the turbo thrusters, none of her usual screaming acceleration for this trip.

"Hold together girl. Just one more run and you can rest. I promise."

She hoped it was a promise she could keep, hoped she wouldn't pass out and plummet to her death as she climbed to cruising altitude, winging towards the Mission on a circuitous route chosen to skirt the dangerous depths of the valley.

Before long, the forest opened to reveal a black glass pyramid flanked by rows of simple, confab houses and larger outbuildings. Reinforced concrete, three meters thick and four meters high, topped with charged wire and defensive weaponry provided a protective barrier to the outside world. Sufficient to keep small groups of antagonistic natives from causing grief, not sufficient when those natives brought their friends and cluster rockets. The place burned.

Alexa came in low, masked by the smoke, and landed behind the rectory. Camouflaging the bike with the plentiful debris, she dispatched half a dozen foraging Jaru before slinking inside the ravaged structure where Father Ryan sprawled in front of his desk, a pile of twisted limbs and shredded black vestments, the top of his head missing. Savages, they'd eaten his brains, probably while he was still alive. Not that she cared; he'd got what was coming to him. Reaped what he sown.

She wedged the door closed and checked out the room. Thrashed. Everything of value, everything portable, stripped away. The Jaru were fast and efficient, she had to give them that.

Activating a well-hidden switch deployed a secret ramp into a dark cellar. She turned on her lights. Shelves crowded with fertility idols, masks, and artwork lined one wall, cages, the other, a stark testament to how the Church operated in the shadows.

Two expensive graphite trunks sat on a pull cart ready to go. Thank heaven for small favours. She towed the cases up and out to the bike, stopping to gun down another small swarm of surprised bugs before taking flight once again. No roundabout route this time. Once she hit cruising altitude she made a beeline for the base.

The mist thinned and she could see the ant-like aliens, masses of them, streaming through the forest. The entire hive? Had to be. The mining ship *Demeter* blew by in a blast of fire, clawing its way into the sky and tearing the air with a series of echoing booms. The miners weren't fools.

Alexa tensed as the base came into view, defensive screens bright and gun turrets firing into the trees, long lines of orange and purple. Puffs of smoke and flashes indicated the Jaru were pushing forward. *Ne ne ne ne ne.* Her sensors indicated a rocket coming in fast. "Shit." Why the hell had she given Ma'la'mor everything in the bloody cargo pod?

The Captain banked hard, deployed countermeasures, and punched the turbo. The bike rolled, indicators wailing. Shit. She'd forgotten about the failed thrusters. The rocket punched through a stabilizer fin, exploding in a ball of fire, the shockwave flipping the bike and sending it into a wild spin. Systems failed. Praying her armour would hold up, she rode the death spiral and plowed into the maintenance deck, skipping and bouncing until smashing into the side of an equipment shed.

Light. Pain. She blinked, surprised to be alive, and tried to wipe the blood from her eyes. One arm didn't respond. From her horizontal and hazy vantage, she saw Zed's Wolverine, no more than a pile of scrap metal, spewing flames and smoke. A ruptured panel fell with a *clang*.

Bing tossed a blanket over the last in a short row of bodies, and limped over. "Welcome back Captain. Just like old times, isn't it?"

"I hate this fucking place," she said, rolling over with a groan. "Let's go, my armour took the worst of it. I'm okay."

"Like hell you are." He dug a pain suppressor from his pocket, looked at her armoured rear end, and pressed it against her neck before heading back to the bodies. "I have news, let me grab a med kit and I'll bring you up to speed."

Zed, looking like he'd bathed in blood, emerged from the inside of the hanger screaming orders to the remaining troopers and maintenance bots. One team rotated a large plasma cannon meant to repel aerial assaults. He saw her and hurried over.

"Captain, Bing said you went to the Mission on your own. What the hell is wrong with you?"

The laugh came out a cough. She spit some frothy blood, and rubbed at her eyes as the sergeant slid out of focus. "They're dead. They're all dead."

He yelled another command at the bots and looked down at her. "Of course, they are. You couldn't possibly rescue them on your bike. What the hell were you thinking?"

Her gaze strayed towards the wreckage, just for a second, but it was enough. Small metal cylinders, the sort that fitted any auto-injector, leaked from a broken case. He bent and picked one up, saw the heart and lightning bolt symbol, and staggered back.

"Blood Lust? You... all this... you," he rasped, unslinging his carbine.

"You don't know shit." She pulled herself up the corrugated shed wall.

"Don't I? It all makes sense. Why we never found the pirates, no matter how hard we looked. Why we kept the Church under our wing."

Bing fumbled through the med kit, tossing items to the ground. He found another injector. "It doesn't matter. Thousands of Jaru are about to swarm this place. A handful of soldiers, one android, and a couple of dozen bots won't last long. Let's get to the ship and escape while we still can."

Zed wasn't listening. He stood, staring at the broken case, shaking his head. "It does matter." He pointed his rifle at the Captain. "You're under arrest."

"Be reasonable, this isn't the time for accusations." said Bing.

"Shut up! You're just as guilty." Zed turned and fired a burst from his wire-cutter, the flechettes stitching a line across Bing's waist before erupting in an explosion of synthetic gore.

Thrum. Zed tottered and collapsed, a smoking hole in his chest. He twitched and she shot him again. Self-righteous bastard. She holstered her pistol, impressed it still worked, impressed anything worked, and dropped to her knees beside the android. He lived, if you could call it that, still struggled. She ran her fingers through his wiry hair until he opened his silver eyes and blinked. Tried to speak. "Ship." The word produced a gushing stream of artificial blood. He twitched and raised an arm, pressed a data card into her hand, pointed towards the upper landing pad where the scout reflected the harsh sunlight. "Ballard. He's..." The hand fell away, the spark blinking out.

Damn it all. He deserved better.

The massive gate protecting the base entrance blew apart with an earth-shattering *boom*. A stream of bugs poured in, met in turn by vaporizing blasts from the plasma cannon. Chaos erupted.

The injector hissed, Blood Lust lightning flooding her with strength, suppressing the fatigue, pain, and returning life to her mangled arm. It might kill her, might kick her over the edge, but it didn't matter. She roared for Suzy. The bot expressed dismay at the two bodies, but obeyed orders to repack the cases and carry them the waiting ship. Anger burned, blocking out Bing's death, Zed's words, and the spotty trail of blood beneath her feet.

The dead android's cracked codes worked like magic and the ships cool, lavender scented air washed over her, invigorating her, exciting her. She traced blood along the smooth walls all the way to the cockpit and sunk into the command chair.

"Ship, power up and plot a course to Odysseus, most direct route, maximum speed."

"Authorization?" The ship queried, a feminine purr.

She slotted the data card. "Sinclair. Captain. C14512022." Lights came on and the floor hummed beneath her feet.

"Hello Lex." An unmistakable voice. Ballard.

She rotated the chair and stared down the corridor, drug infused colour leaking from her face. The Major leaned against a bulkhead wall; blood and bio-gel leaking from a mass of crudely affixed bandages, a regeneration mask covering an eye, ear, and the top of his head. He held a large power pistol.

"Jon. You're..."

"Alive? Here? You look like you've seen a ghost." He swayed and strained to balance himself with a thickly swathed arm. "Not happy to see me?"

"Yes. Of course." Her tone didn't match her words.

"Bullshit. Tisiphone, please belay that last order, and any other from Captain Sinclair. Set a course to Newton and inform Command I've completed my investigation. Tell them I'm on route with the suspected drug smuggler."

"No!"

Ballard waved his gun. "I wanted to believe you were innocent, that you didn't actually know what the hell was going on. Even after your troopers confirmed my suspicion about your fling with W'yn'ea's son, even when Prince Ma'la'mor attacked when he couldn't possibly know I was on planet, and especially when Zed, after he'd found me, patched me up, and dragged me back here, spilled about your secretive and suspect behaviour. I still wanted to believe." Scarlet and cobalt dripped and pattered onto the deck.

"It's not that simple."

"Maybe, but here you are, in the middle of a battle, hijacking my ship and setting course to a planet well known for dealing in illicit drugs. There are two cases of Blood Lust sitting in the corridor, for god's sake. What am I supposed to think?"

"Jon." She grimaced, the slew of chemicals twisting her between rage and determination. "You *owe* me. I disobeyed direct orders, ruined my career to save your life. Don't do this. Save mine."

"I am."

The ship lurched, forcing the Major to shift position to keep from falling. His aim wavered for a moment, an eternity. Alexa snapped her pistol out and fired, watched her old lover slide to floor in a heap, light fading from his eyes, life leaking away. More blood on her hands. She'd killed them all, friend and enemy, sent them all to the hell she was been dragged into, kicking and screaming.

Another explosion rocked the ship as it struggled to lift off, obeying Ballard's final orders. Alarms blared and flashing monitors indicated the cargo bay door was damaged and ajar.

"Tisiphone, button up and make for Odysseus."

"Unable to comply Captain Sinclair. Course set for Newton, arrival in eight standard days."

"No, I don't think so," she hissed, returning to command chair and picking up the data card, fingers tingling. There must be a portable comp kicking around, one she could use to tweak the cracker program and reset her access before the ship got to the transit point. She hadn't come this far to give up now.

Feet pattered across deck plating.

"Intruders have damaged the air lock beyond my current self-restoration capability. Please eliminate and begin manual repairs at once."

Shit. "How many? Weapons?"

"I detect seventeen Jaru drones, five armed with power weapons."

Her pistol displayed an error code, tapped out. Double shit. She scooped up Ballard's and crouched behind the command chair. Checked its charge. One percent. One bloody percent. Maybe enough to kill something if you held it against their head. Maybe.

The bugs reached the corridor outside the bridge and paused at Ballard's body. They wouldn't kill her, at least not until they'd peeled her head like an orange and sucked out her brain. Not going to happen. She hefted the pistol, feeling it's comfortable weight, raised it.

Boom, another fucking disaster.

11

The Dragons Eye

Scott snatched up my yellow cats-eye with the hairline crack. "You lose again bozo. Winner takes all."

"Asshole." I muttered under my breath.

"What did you say, dork?" Scott was a big, wide shouldered farm boy with short straw hair and angry green eyes. I didn't want to antagonize him. He ruled grade six, and had a tendency to bring misery on those he disliked. I was on the borderline.

"Nothing. Just cursing my luck."

"You should." He turned his ball cap forward and dropped the marbles, my marbles, into a bulging leather drawstring sack. Another boy, Casey, came over and slapped his shoulder. "Bozo loses again eh? He never learns."

It was the same old story, only this time I was finished. I'd literally lost all my marbles. I could spend my allowance on more, but what was the point? I'd be throwing away money. It was like Charlie Brown and the football. I just wanted to run away and yell "Aaugh!"

That evening at dinner my father noticed my brooding. "You look like someone just ran over your dog. What's wrong?"

"I suck at marbles. I lost my last one at recess today."

"Ah." He understood. The game had been a staple when he was a child. "I'll see if I can find some steelies at work tomorrow. They're better than glass any day. The extra weight gives them a lot of power."

I brightened. Steelies. Small ball bearings the same size of as marbles but way cooler. They were rare, prized, and expensive, at least compared to glass.

The next evening, as I finished my homework, dad dropped a handful of silver spheres onto my desk. "Here you go. Now cheer up." He mussed my hair, stopping when he realized his hands were still stained with grease.

A dozen perfect steel marbles, I was back in the game. "Thanks Dad!"

"You're welcome." He turned to leave then stopped and felt around in his jacket pocket. "I have one more, a bit damaged, but it might work okay." He tossed me the largest ball bearing I'd ever seen, close to an inch across. Heavy. It wasn't as shiny as the other ones, more grey and black, with a series of orange mottles. "I pulled it out of one of giant pumps in the old part of the factory. The housing was just a mound of melted slag from the fire last year but this guy survived with minor damage." I thanked him again and he smiled, tweaked my nose, and headed out to start on the chores.

The large bearing was an odd beast, warm where the others were cold, dark where the others were bright, full of personality, full of potential. I placed it on the desk, in the pencil groove between the other dozen, and went back to my homework. Struggling with some algebraic expressions, I saw movement from the corner of my eye. The small steelies quivered, the ones on the left shifting in tiny jerks further to the left, while the ones on the right inching further to the right. They strained away from their larger brother in the middle. I picked up the big one and the others stopped moving. I put it back and they quivered again. Weird. It must have some kind of repulsive magnetic charge. I prodded it with loose change to no effect. Strange behaviour though, I'd have to ask my dad about it. I finished up, tossed all thirteen into an empty crown royal bag, and went to bed.

❖❖❖

The next morning, I came into the schoolyard with my head held high, proud, dangerous, a gunslinger with new pistols. I hung around outside the circle and watched the action for a while.

Scott wandered by. "Feeling left out loser?"

"Not really. Just checking out who has some nice gems." I shook my bag. "Time to start taking back."

He laughed in my face. "Ha! You wish. You're the worst player I've ever seen."

"I'm feeling lucky today. I guess we'll see."

"Yeah, I guess. Come find me when you want to add to my collection."

I waited before making my move, measuring my chances against each gladiator. The easiest mark was Lorne Williams, the tiny bespectacled nerd with the silly grin on his face. He played at my level but seemed to have money to burn, showing up each week with yet another pocketful of glass.

I pulled out the steelies, their distinctive polished glow and unique clatter drawing every boy in the vicinity. The vultures circled to watch another disaster unfold. It was a spectacle all right, just not the kind they'd imagined. I didn't just beat Lorne, I crushed him, the steelies performing beyond my greatest expectations, blasting his marbles out of the ring with pinpoint accuracy and terrible force.

Kids talked. My victory was just a fluke they said, a one-time luck streak that wouldn't be repeated. Everyone was hungry for an opportunity to snag easy loot and it didn't take long for the first of the challengers to step up. I took on all comers, and destroyed them. Every last one of them. I couldn't lose. They examined my untouchable spheres thinking they were loaded or something, but the end verdict was that I had just scored one hell of a hot streak. For the first time, ever, I went home with my bag half full. I glowed with victory, glowed with superiority.

I got up early to go through my replenished collection and sort out the gems from the common. Only ten of the steelies, plus the big one, rolled out on the carpet. I thought back to the previous day, retracing my steps. The bag hadn't left my sight. I turned it inside out, probed every seam. No holes or damage. That left just one suspect.

My little brother screwed up his face when I accused him at breakfast. "Why would I want your stupid marbles?"

"I can think of a dozen reasons. The important one being that they're mine."

He flicked fruit loops at me, spinning them across the table and onto the floor where the dog snapped them up. "I didn't take your stuff. Trust me. If I wanted to mess with you I'd poop in your—."

Our mother's hand slapped the table. "Language."

He giggled and gargled a glass of milk.

I believed him. Mostly. He was a real shit when he wanted to torment me.

❖❖❖

The day turned out to be even more successful than the last, boys and girls lining up to take me down and end my reign of terror. One by one they fell to my matchless skill. Kids who had never spoken a kind word wanted to be my friend and learn my secrets. My steelies ruled all. But only mine. Guessing it was the secret of my success, other ball bearings appeared from the bottom of toolboxes, various pieces of machinery, or in one case, stolen from the local automotive supply shop. It made no difference.

I ended the day with enough spoils to require a second bag and giddily split my collection so the metals were in one and the glass in another. That night I carefully counted and sorted. Twenty-eight steelies plus the giant one, and I still had two more days till summer break.

Before I went to sleep I took the big one out and held it for a bit. In the dark, with just the glow of the night-light, it looked like an eye. A Dragon's Eye. Rage filled. Savage. What else could survive a fire?

❖❖❖

When I crawled out of bed the next morning I did a quick check to make sure my brother hadn't been vindictive during the night. No poop anywhere I could see or smell, but the bag felt lighter. I trembled and knew without looking what I'd find. Nine! Just nine remained when I dumped them on the bed. "Son of a..." I glanced at the door, praying my mother wasn't in earshot. Vibrating and seeing red, I ran to my brother's room. He was

sound asleep, peaceful under Asia posters and
dangling models of World War Two fighter jets. I
punched him the stomach as hard as I could. He
woofed, tumbled out of bed, and lay on the floor
heaving. My mom walked in just as I was lining up
to hit him again. She grabbed my arm. "Just what
do you think are you doing?"

"He stole them."

My brother opened his eyes and glared. "I
didn't steal anything."

"Right..." I said as I pulled myself out of her grip
and fled to my room. Right.

Mom followed me. "You go right back and say
you're sorry. Even if he did take something, you
can't go around hitting people. Do you want to be
a bully?"

I looked at the floor. "Sorry."

"Say that to him, not me. I'll think of some
punishment. It's going to take more than 'Sorry' to
make this right. Just be glad your dad wasn't here."

Dad. Yeah, his disappointed look was worse
than any punishment mom could come up with.

I wandered back to my brother's room and
mumbled a semi-heartfelt apology. He had
daggers in his eyes and something else, the sort of
hurt look a puppy gives you when you punish it

for something it didn't do. But he had, I was sure of it.

After that fiasco, a strange day at school. Instead of line-ups to dethrone the champion, avoidance. The boys put their heads together, whispered, and avoided eye contact as I passed by. I spent recess alone, drawing circles in the dirt.

❖❖❖

Friday, the last day of school for the year and my final day at Centennial Elementary School. In the Fall, I'd be off to a larger middle school on the other side of town, new faces and fewer bullies with any luck. I needed to look on the bright side.

Scott came over as I was eating lunch and cleaning out my locker. He stood, staring, but didn't say anything for a few moments. "You don't look like a cheater. You look like a loser. Your luck runs out today. Final recess, back field, be there. Winner takes all. And I mean everything." He hefted his bulging leather sack and smacked it against my locker door.

There was a crowd at the field when I showed up. Scott had drawn the circle already and stood there with unequalled bravado. He held up a huge sparkling steelie, almost equal to mine. "You're not the only one with a big gun. Let's do it."

I reached into my bag and stopped cold. My fingers found just two smaller bearings along with the big one. I'd slept with the bag, just to ensure my brother couldn't get his hands on it. Maybe there was a hole? No, I'd checked it each day. I wanted to scream, to smash something, but choked away my rage and dug out a few emerald cats-eyes from my spoils to make up the half dozen I needed.

This game did not go like the others. A struggle. A battle royale. I still had the two steelies that couldn't miss, but the cats-eyes were cursed. It came down to the wire.

Scott yelped and pumped his arm when his shot knocked the last of mine out of the circle. I brought out the big gun, the Dragon's Eye, and polished it with my sleeve. The sight of it brought whispers from the assembly. Scott looked at it and grinned. He reckoned it would be his soon enough. My aim was true, and I blasted all his remaining crystals out of the ring. That left only his own heavyweight. He bent, knuckles to the ground and flicked, the bearing flying toward mine with uncanny precision. I closed my eyes at the last second, not wanting to see.

I didn't hear it connect. In fact, there was dead silence until someone gasped. Then I heard Scott.

He sounded pissed. "Where'd it go?" When I opened my eyes, I could still see the Eye where it rested, but Scott's shooter was nowhere to be seen. He walked around, looking for it, his fists bunched. It was gone, vanished. He came over and looked down at me.

"Hand it over."

I shrugged and opened my hands. "It wasn't me." He shoved and I stumbled back, falling. Before I could stand he was on me, pounding away in fury. I protected my face but there wasn't much I could do. He was twice as big, and strong as an ox. As the blows fell I had a moment of clarity about what I had done to my brother that morning. I wasn't like Scott. Was I?

Then the weight was gone. Lorne, Casey and some other boys pulled Scott off and pinned him to the ground, sitting on him until he cooled off. He lay in the grass for a minute, eyes closed, before letting out a long pent up breath. Then he clambered up, walked over, and dropped his leather sack at my feet. "Enjoy your moment in the sun hotshot." He looked smaller, weaker.

The Dragon's Eye felt warm in my hand and my fear burned away. I'd won. I'd beaten him. Next year I'd be king of the schoolyard, a new schoolyard. Next year I'd be the Dragon.

ROBERT BOSE

12

Fallen

Twisitoria Alegeiun Caliaster sprawled on the abbey roof naked, golden scales soaking up the warm sun. She stretched and let her wings unfurl, wings of tiny brass feathers, wings broken in her fall from the heavens. They called her an angel, but she wasn't, not really. She was a creature of the air, a creature of the sky, a descendant of the righteous, before war divided the servants of god, before war split darkness from light. More machine than human, the Church said, though she could pass for a young girl. Except for the wings, of course. Her beautiful wings. Her wretched wings.

Out on the horizon, clouds gathered, dark and cold. She hated the cold, hated the dark. She dreamt of dancing above the clouds, where the sun shone eternal, where her family once dwelt, but they were lost. Forever lost. While she loved her new family, the doting Abbess, the clockworks who defended her from enemies of God, she longed to escape her comfortable prison, longed to spread her wings and soar, longed to be free.

The wind picked up and she shivered, sliding into her tunic, and watched the storm roll in, white-capped waves racing across the bay to hammer the rocky shoreline. Riding the leading crest was a ship, a ship with no sail, plowing hard towards the dock tucked away in the harbour below. She'd heard of such ships, all iron and steam, fire and thunder.

The storm hit, and with it another kind of power, one she loved as much as the sun. Excited, she popped to her feet, scampered up the tiles, and put one hand on the thick copper steeple. Cascading sheets of lightning ravaged the old church, scorching the long terracotta tiles and igniting an exposed wooden brace where the roofing had fallen away. She reached out and tapped the surging energy, drinking the power, savouring its purity. Her long blonde hair billowed up and out, each strand writhing with a life of its own.

The storm smashed against the rocky shore and stopped, churning, caught as some force held it in check while the lightning continued, waves upon waves of it, blasting the steeple and her arching body. Too much, too fast. Her broken brass wings, bursting with energy, struggled to lift her, unable to catch the wind but unwilling to give up trying.

A tall woman in white robes poked her head out of an adjacent dormer. The Abbess. "Twist. No! This is... there is danger here. You've taken too much, you must stop before—"

Twist held up her free hand, ignoring the command, and sang. A white-gold song of life and love, of sea and air, the heavens above, the depths below. Strong words. Pure words.

"Caligavit." The loud, harsh spell produced a faint barrier around the child, dimming and calming, drawing down the charge, dissipating the bonds of power. Shaking her head, the Abbess gave Twist a stern look and beckoned. "Come now, the guardians wait below. A great darkness approaches and we must find shelter if we are to weather this storm."

The still glowing Twist, eyes dancing, nodded and slid into her teacher's open arms. The Abbess hugged her, kissing the top of her head, and after a moment, hugged her again. They made their way down through the labyrinth of abandoned and forgotten stairwells, hand in hand, until they reached the nave. *Boom*. An echo. *Booooom*. The high vaulted chamber shook, fine dust drifting from the ceiling, the electric candelabras sparking and flickering.

Mark stomped into the room, an amber blur of motors and cogs. He barred the wide double doors with a thick timber beam as smoke poured from the blackened brass plates armouring his torso.

"Abbess." The machine bent a knee. "A determined intruder has entered the grounds searching for..." He looked to the Abbess and down at Twist. "He has destroyed the guardians and has proven himself an adversary beyond my ability to deter."

"I see." She gave Twist one last hug, touching the girl's cheek with a pale hand. "Please take Twist into the deepest vault, the one with the silver door. I will secure the abbey and come for you once the dem... once the intruder has been dealt with." *Boom*. The older woman wrapped herself in light and stood before the splintering barrier. "Go! Go now."

Mark scooped Twist up and roared into the vestry, through a hidden trapdoor, and into the musty basement. *Boom*. Explosions whispered above. Twist heard a shout, heard the rending of wood and iron, the shriek of flesh. The Abbess? No, the Abbess was strong, a shield against the darkness, a shield that couldn't break.

Down. Faster. Further. Past the furnace and steam engine that powered the complex. Past walls of pipe that pulled cold water from the ocean. Past shelves of casks, shelves of dusty bottles, not forgotten, but waiting for a day of celebration, one that had never come. Endless stairs led to a wide stone hallway, and at the end, a tarnished silver door. It opened with a squeal.

Twist tapped Mark's shoulder. "Can we wait for her here?"

"No. The directive was precise. We must seek safety behind the wards."

"Please. We can't leave her." Twist squirmed out of his grasp and dropped to the ground.

The machine picked her back up. "We must continue. We must–"

She sang, a simple song this time. Short. Poignant. This song had power, the power to influence, to bend will. It was, of course, a forbidden song, but one she used to get her own way, more often than naught. Mark listened and turned back towards sub-basement and watched the proximity light spells fade one by one. They threw a fragmented pattern across his damaged face.

After a time, the lights flared to life and a figure strode towards them. It wasn't the Abbess, but a tall man in a full-length black leather coat. Heavy gloves. Square top hat. Ruby goggles. The man stopped, touching fingers together in an exaggerated display. "How thoughtful of you to wait. Please hand over the child and I will be on my way without further... unpleasantries."

Mark tossed Twist through the doorway. "Seal the door," he urged. "I will delay him."

"No, I won't leave you." She took a step forward.

"You must." Oil dripped onto stone. "Please Twist, just this once, do as I request. Please..." Her guardian clenched his battered fists and stalked towards the smiling stranger.

Please. A hopeless word. A desperate word. A word Mark used when he'd exhausted all other options with her. Twist pushed the door shut, watching ruby light bath the corridor. Who was this man? What did he want with her? *Boom*. The door shook, a mighty blow repulsed by ancient wards. She sang a song of light and marveled, fear and concern overwhelmed by wonder. The vault wasn't the stuffy tomb she'd imagined, it was a vast cavern, one carved by the sea, stalactites dripping and stalagmites thrusting,

"The figure stopped and smiled, touching fingers together
in an exaggerated display."

a natural amphitheater presenting a performance for the ages. *Boom*. A long, slender spike of rock dropped and exploded, showering her with wet fragments. Another snapped and shattered nearby.

She felt a cold aura penetrate the door, an aura of darkness, of death, and she knew in her heart that both her teacher and protector had fallen, as her mother had when the lofty pinnacles of Leukai had collapsed into the sea so many years ago. Hands became shaking fists. She wanted to rip open the door, sing a song, make the stranger pay. She reached out.

Boom. The cold chilled her bones and she snatched her hand back. No. Not here. Not now. This was something beyond her. Something old. Something evil. *Boom*. The chamber shook, the entire ceiling cracking with the scream of tortured stone. At the far end, where her light faded, the mouth of a tunnel gaped an invitation. Tunnels. The Abbess had mentioned the tunnels under the old church, tunnels used to evacuate the priests from the nearby town of Avranches in times of war. She could use them to reach the sanctuary of the cathedral there. The Bishop would help her, would know what to do. She darted across the chamber, dodging the raining stone, and entered a narrow passageway as the cavern collapsed in a grinding roar. The tunnel became a labyrinth. Twisted. Meandering. She pressed on, tiring, feeling the walls closing in on her. Smothering her.

When she was about to give up hope, about to succumb to the crushing dark, stairs, crooked winding stairs that took her up, way up into the catacombs beneath the cathedral. She passed through crypts, trailing hands across dusty inscriptions, past niches filled with cobwebbed skulls, past coffins bearing the seal of the Templars.

A door blocked her way, a door of beaten red brass with the bas-relief of harp and book, the border etched with arcane sigils. She knocked three times, the proper number, and waited. When the door didn't open, she knocked thrice more, as hard as she could, the brass ringing like a bell. No one came. She stood there, song light casting long shadows, shivering, trembling. She didn't know the song for opening this sort of door, so she sat down, hugged her legs to her chest, and leaned against the cool metal. Waited.

A hand shook her awake and round amber eyes peered into hers. "Twisitoria? Was that you knocking?" The eyes looked around, saw she was alone. "Yes, of course it was."

"Deacon! I wasn't sure you heard." She hopped up and gave the clockwork man a hug.

"Just now an initiate informed me of an infernal racket coming from the catacombs, they thought the dead were waking. I've been busy helping secure the cathedral from an approaching storm. Why did you take the under-road? Why are you here alone?"

"I need to see the Bishop. Right now. Something terrible has happened." She rubbed warmth into her arms. "The Abbe–"

He put a finger to her lips. "Now, now, I'm sure it can't be that bad. Follow, the Bishop is busy, but I will take you to him."

They climbed out of the basement, through expansive halls crowded with singing monks, the hallmark of the Avranches Cathedral. Deacon brought her upstairs to a sitting room stuffed with books and maps.

He wrapped her in a woolen blanket. "Wait here, I'll inform the Bishop."

Twist poked impatiently through the books, most containing songs and hymns of the mundane variety. She studied a map spanning a wall, sliding a finger down the Apennine Peninsula until she found the Ionian Sea and the spot where the spires of Leukai had thrust from the water, her home before the world had come crashing down. Nothing remained except an empty spot. To punctuate the point, thunder *boomed* and the room rattled.

The door creaked open and the Bishop entered, his black and red robe, billowing and rustling. "Twist, what a pleasure to see you. I hear you've come alone and that something terrible has happened. Is that true?" The old man sat down and eyed her intently.

The girl turned and nodded. "The storm brought a ship and a stranger. A man, dark and cold, who forced his way in and..." She looked at her feet and twisted her hands.

"It's okay child, tell me."

"He killed them."

The Bishop rose to his feet, face ashen. "What! Are you sure?"

She nodded, lip trembling.

"Sit, tell me everything." *Boom*. More thunder.

When she finished her short tale, he frowned. "So, he was looking for you." He tapped his chin. "What did he look like?"

"Tall, square, dressed like a prince, his eyes masked by ruby goggles."

The Bishop grew even more pale. "Ruby goggles, by the heavens... wait here." He rushed from the room and returned with a thick book bound in mottled black leather. Leafing through the colourful illustrations, he stopped at a page and held it up. It depicted the figure from the Abbey. "Did he look like this?"

She shivered again, despite the blanket. "Yes."

The Bishop slammed the book shut and yelled for Deacon, whispering into the machine's ear. Deacon shook and hurried off.

"Who is he?" Twist asked.

"It's best you not know." The Bishop turned and clasped his hands behind his back, began to pace the room. "An ancient evil, one long forgotten."

"Why would he be looking for me?"

His forehead creased and he didn't reply.

"Please, tell me." She started to hum the forbidden song, the song that bent minds and loosened tongues.

"Stop Twist," he said, shaking his head and rubbing the silver cross that hung from his neck. "You know you can't sing that—" A tremendous blast of thunder shook the cathedral, drowning her out, as Deacon reappeared.

"Your Grace, he's at the doors and demands we hand over the child at once."

"Have you assembled the host?"

A nod. "Those with the will, the skill, to resist are waiting in the Nave. The rest have fled to the catacombs."

"Excellent. Stay here with Twist while we expel this fiend."

Twist grasped the Bishop's robe, digging her fingers in. "Please, don't leave me here! Let me see. Let me help."

Deacon gently pried her away. "It will be fine, child," he said, holding her tight.

She struggled as the Bishop strode out the door, slamming it closed. "No, it won't," she whispered.

Repeated cracks of thunder shook the room. *Boom. Boom. BOOM.* The sounds of tearing metal, just like at the Abbey. She squirmed, feeling cold, feeling trapped, she needed to get out before it all happened again. "Deacon, let me go."

The clockwork man shook his head. "I cannot."

Again, she sang, this time without interruption. Deacon relaxed his grip and she wiggled free, opening the door and peeking out. Voices, loud, angry, echoed down the hall.

Boom. She crept down the corridor, Deacon in tow, to the balcony that overlooked the Nave and peered between the railing slats. The great doors of the cathedral hung in ruin, smoking. Between them stood the dark stranger. A wall of light blocked his way, projected by a crowd of priest and monks. The Bishop stood in their midst, staff of office thrust before him.

The stranger gestured, hands open. "Come now Julien, be reasonable. Give me what I want or see all you know brought to ruin."

"She is a child of God, and under his protection. I say again, be gone demon, you sully this place with your taint." Golden stars flew from the staff to surround the stranger, wrapping him in an amber cocoon.

The man laughed. "So be it." His goggles flared and ruby lightning sprayed across the room, scything through the wall of light, through the priests and monks, and finally through the Bishop. Bodies fell, crackling with energy, until all was quiet. The dark man looked up to the balcony, looked right at Twist. "Ah, there you are."

❖❖❖

The sun cast diamond shadows across her white tunic. Twist tried to catch them as they shifted with the light breeze, but they slipped through her fingers, ephemeral as always. So close that time. So close. Her cage, a copper pendulum at the bottom of a chain rising to the great arch above the high castle terrace, swayed, buffeted by a gust of wind, the precursor to the daily storm she'd come to fear.

"Good afternoon Twisitoria, ready for another?"

Twist remained silent, staring at the dark stranger.

"I will take that as a yes." The man clipped one end of a bundle of braided copper wire to the bottom of the cage and the other to a fist sized black cube, set within the crenel of a nearby parapet. The cube throbbed, emanating intense cold.

She mustered the strength for a song and let it all out, directed towards the wretched creature that kept her trapped. A song stained with sadness, of sorrow, a compulsion, a demand to free her, a song ending in his death, drained of will and begging for the underworld.

Except it didn't. He continued to work on his mechanism, oblivious to the curse that surrounded him, just as he had during each previous attempt.

"Now," he said at last, as the rain began to fall and lightning flayed the terrace, "give me your power."

Each strike rang against the cage, flowing into her, charging her, filling her with power. Before long she began to glow. First white-gold, then white-blue, and finally as the full force of nature pressed down, white-red. Another song, this one involuntary. Raw. Unfettered. She screamed, the amplified energy now forced back into the cage, through the cable, and into the cube.

"Yes. Yes!" The man pressed himself against the castle wall, hands raised to the heavens, a rippling shield providing an island of calm amid the violence. "More!"

For the sixth straight day, Twist, exhausted and spent, sputtered, empty, and slipped into unconsciousness.

❖❖❖

The dark man returned to perform his morning ritual, a sharp intonation of the classic "Nova Initia." A spell of preservation, of renewal, that alleviated her need to eat, drink, or concern herself with other bodily needs besides sleep.

"Why?"

The bright sun glinted off ruby lenses. "A good question. Do you truly want to know the answer?"

She nodded.

He pulled off his coat and shirt, revealing a sculpted chest of black copper skin. The symbol of God, a double starburst etched in silver, dominated his right breast. A rough hole pierced his left. She could see all the way through. Gears turned and cogs spun. He had no heart.

Twist choked back a gasp. "Dantanian!" A mighty servant of God, a living machine, torn from above and cast to earth when the companions of Abaddon failed in their treachery. "The Abbess once told me a story. A metal man. The bringer of storms. The Fallen."

"True. All of it." The angelic clockwork, nine parts legend, did up his shirt and straightened his coat. "A good story, one I wrote ages past to tell the truth, but one lacking a satisfactory ending. With your... assistance dear cousin, my long banishment is almost at an end. One more storm, one more charge, and I will regain the strength I need to reclaim my place in the heavens. My brother renews the fight and I must join him."

"Cousin?" Her eyes went wide.

"Of a sort. You think the Almighty would sully his hands creating your kind? The basic design, yes, but I did the work. Those eyes. Those scales. Those pretty little wings. A pale imitation of my own."

Twist shook her head. "I don't believe you."

He ignored her. "When I heard Abaddon's call I sought out the sky singing sisters of golden

Thelxiepeia. Only they possessed the power magnification I required. But I was too late. The world grows old, you see, old and tired. The lofty towers of Leukai, no longer buoyed by the dimming sun, fell into the sea. I despaired, the only other sister dwelt far to the east, at the top of the world, unassailable even by one such as myself." Dantanian paused and tapped the cage. "Then I heard about a broken little bird, found floating in the Ionian Sea, wrapped in her dead mother's arms. A winged child spirited away by the Church and sequestered in a remote abbey. You."

❖❖❖

A massive spike of lightning lashed down. The most powerful yet. Twist clung to the bottom of the cage, a conduit between heaven and earth, and felt her life slip away, drawn little by little into the cold black heart. It glowed like a dark sun. Pulsing. Beating.

Dantanian shouted into the storm. "Everything! Give me everything."

Her stomach growled and her lips grew dry. The restorative magic infusing her began to fail, frayed by the torrent of nature. Energy warped the air and she could see the residual threads of the spell struggling to maintain integrity. Layered under its dissolving web were traces of an older spell, the shield the Abbess had graced her with on the roof of the abbey, burned away in all but pattern. An idea sparked. Maybe, just maybe, there was a way to use it. She sang through clenched teeth and bleeding lips, a tiny song that pulled the strands of one spell into the image of the other, weaving them together to create an insulating shell around her fraying form.

Dantanian didn't notice. He'd left the shelter of the castle wall and stood over the heart, his laughter mimicking the thunder.

She held herself together but it wasn't enough, she needed to fly, if only a little and for long enough to break the connection. Her wings were useless, the delicate frames broken in her fall, the tiny crystal feathers torn or lost. The Church had tried to fix them, but they lacked the knowledge, the skill for such intricate work. More power arced over her golden scales. The storm would soon crest and Twist knew she would not survive. She must fly. Did she need her wings? She was a creature of the air. A creature of light. Of song.

So, Twist sang her favourite. A song of life and love, of sea and air, the heavens above, the depths below. It cut across the terrace, washing out the storm, washing away the terrible laughter. She sang faster, harder, pulling in the lightning, transforming it as it transformed her. The air around her blurred and she floated. Not high, but enough. The connection to the cube broke with a thunderclap.

Dantanian leapt down from the crenel and raced to the cage. Twist opened her wings and drew in even more power, glowing white, and used it to strengthen the spell holding her together. This was the pure power God's treacherous creation had desired. When she couldn't contain anymore she let the excess go in one tremendous burst. *Boooooom*. The cage vaporized, spraying burning copper across the terrace, the force blasting the still beating heart off the parapet and into the ocean below. Dantanian picked himself up, his cloak in shreds and one ruby eye cracked. Without a sound, or backward glance, he ran to the edge and hurled himself into the depths.

The storm died. An eerie calm settled. Whispering the song now, her throat raw, body ravaged, Twist released her cloak of celestial energy and collapsed to the ground. She'd done it. Free. But to what end? Everything she knew, she held dear, was gone. Destroyed by a mad, revenge bent machine, a machine she was certain would follow her to the ends of the earth. The ends of the earth... Yes, that was it.

She didn't have much of a head start, had no idea where she was, but Twisitoria Alegeiun Caliaster staggered into the castle and down endless stairs, humming a new song.

13

The Sharp Edge
of the Moon

The moon lanced the night. It drove silver blades through dark, angry clouds, cutting here and slicing there, sending cold forged light to snuff the shadows and cleave the veil between this world and the next.

Oblivious to the supernatural implications, but entangled just the same, Marco ran, ran hard. He followed the light, sprinting from patch to patch, until he reached the cenotaph in Central Memorial Park, a looming monument of weathered grey stone radiating death and despair. A terrible place to stop, open and exposed, but his chest heaved, threatening to explode, and his pants rode low.

The weary bro rested hands on knees and puked, hacking up a lung and the remains of dinner. Shit. He should be chilling at the frat house, guzzling Coors, and slapping ass, instead of tossing up a plate of chicken fried rice with the grim reaper nipping at his heels. Marco scanned the wide courtyard and the nearby gardens, shivering, his adrenaline-fueled high fading fast. No sign of the crazy. Maybe the feral lunatic had found another midnight nomad to turn into a ten finger Happy Meal.

Fuck Ty. Fuck that asshole to hell and back. Worst. Friend. Ever. Sure, the girl they'd found walking along the path had been a sweet little thing, but dammit, not worth dying over. Shit, not even worth slowing down for. Ty had been fixated, almost desperate, for some reason. Maybe it was the full moon. Marco had heard stories about people going a little crazy when it was out, and tonight's was a big one, the biggest he'd ever seen. Whatever the reason, he'd tried to steer Ty clear of trouble, tried to focus him on their quest for weed, but his friend wouldn't listen.

Owooooo. Ogopogo.

Shit, shit, shit. What the hell was that? Marco took a deep breath and busted ass around the cenotaph; heedless when his ball cap caught the air to spin away, heedless when his pants slid further.

"Bum a smoke?"

A ragged figure sprawled across a park bench, long black hair askew, eyes glowing with inner fire. Fuck. Marco leapt two feet into the air, heart pounding, to face plant into the etched concrete walkway. Sweat and tobacco curled out like questing fingers to paw at his pockets.

"A smoke. Got any? I need to warm the bones from the inside tonight."

"God, you gave me a... a fucking heart attack asshole." Marco crawled over to a heavy planter and heaved himself up, gasping and gurgling, blood leaking from his nose and making an ugly mess of his *No Fear* t-shirt. He wiped his face with his arm, flicked away the crimson gore and vomit, and squinted at the ragtag man. The dude, a full blood native, looked a hundred years old, copper skin glowing like vintage leather.

"You must have a smoke. I'll trade you... I got something here you need." A wide smile.

"I don't have any smokes you crazy fucking Indian, and I wouldn't give you one if I did. Jesus, don't you have anything better to do than scare the crap out of people in the middle of the night?"

The old man shrugged and crossed his outstretched legs. Scratched his ear. "Your funeral."

Marco considered that last comment as he hiked up his pants and sprinted down empty streets, dodging a solitary cab, to the Double W Pawn Shop. Not his funeral. Not tonight. He wanted to go home, chalk up what happened to karma, but he couldn't. He had an obligation to his friends and once he had a gun, a big fucking gun, he'd be the one planting bodies.

The shop was closed and dark. Marco circled to the alley and pounded on the reinforced steel door marked Exit Only. No answer. Kicked. Kicked again, sprawling on his back when the opening door smashed into him, a heavy boot catching him in the ribs and a double-barreled shotgun jamming into his stomach deep enough to touch his spine. The massive, muscled arm holding the gun was black and crawling with ink. Winston.

Marco held up shaking hands. "Win, my man. It's just me." He sucked in a breath and spit onto the broken pavement. "You said if I was ever in trouble, real trouble, to come here, day or night, and you'd help. I know you still owe my mom for that alibi and I'm collecting."

The gun pulled away and Winston grunted. "Dammit Marco, I remember, but you gotta call if you're going bust in like this. I just about tore you a new one."

"Lost my phone."

"Bad news." Winston lifted the bro to his feet and brushed him off. "Come on in, just having a brew and watching late night."

Marco ducked under Winston's arm as the ex-football linebacker slammed and locked the door, following the big man through a labyrinth of shrink-wrapped pallets until they reached a crowded office, the walls plastered with faded vintage movie posters. A flat screen TV, showing a crazy looking game show, hung from the ceiling between Escape from New York and Big Trouble in Little China. Winston pulled a couple of cans out of a mini-fridge and tossed Marco one before settling in behind a desk buried in pizza boxes. "What brings you to the Shop in the middle of the night? Shouldn't you be at some dumb-shit party with your retard friends?"

Marco cracked the Bud and gulped it down, flooding his system with liquid determination. "I need to take care of someone first. Have a piece I can borrow? Or buy, I'm good for it."

"Ha!" Winston's laugh boomed. "Give *you* a piece? You got to be fucking kidding me. You'd blow your dick off and the cops would come poking around." He watched Marco's face twist and noticed the blood and puke for the first time. "Shit, you're serious."

"Bloody vengeance serious."

"Look kid, I know all about *bloody vengeance*, but you need to go home, sleep it off, and think hard about it. Once you off someone, there's no going back. If it's a time-sensitive matter, go round up your bros. I'm sure Tyrone would love nothing better than to lay down an ass kicking. Where's the little prick anyways?"

"He's dead. I think. Look Win..." Marco took a long slug of beer and collapsed onto a folding chair, bouncing his head against the wall. "Ty and Morgan, they're both fucking dead so stop with the god damn lecture."

Winston raised an eyebrow. "You're shitting me."

"Look at me! Do you think I tripped or something?"

"Calm down kid. I'm just surprised is all; you three are big on talk and short on action. Drugs or women?"

Marco slid deep into his chair, squeezing his can until it collapsed with a spine-snapping crunch. "Kinda both." He considered, deflating. "No. Way more fucked up than that. Way more–"

"I get it. Fucked up. Spill."

"Fine. We were on our way from Sing-Sing Sam's to see one of the D man's minions, score some weed, when we found this chick in the park by the river. Ty was getting it on, you know how he can be when he's drunk, when this crazy, feral dude showed up. Charged out of bushes like some red-rage fueled tornado. Fucked Ty up in about three seconds, tore him apart, and bit off his ear. His fucking ear!" Marco threw up his arms, splashing beer. "Morgan stuck the dude and the hairy bastard didn't even blink. I... laid a beating on him, a solid beating, but... no way I could deal, so I skipped out while he was chewing off Morgan's fingers one by one."

Winston tossed his can across the room. It bounced off the wall and dropped into a box to join its cousins. "Feral, hairy, with a taste for fingers. Sounds like you boys ran into a grade-a werewolf."

"A what?"

"Shit. Don't you read books? Watch TV?"

"Stop messing with me, I mean it, werewolves aren't real."

"Oh, they're real. Not common, mind you, but they show up in town now and again. Come down out of the mountains from BC. Wu, learn the boy."

Winston walked over to rack of DVD's and started rummaging.

A shock of wild white hair poked from a mound of blankets entombing a brown leather recliner. "Leave me out of this, I'm trying to meditate."

"You woke up when the kid pounded on the door. I know you've been listening. Marco needs to know what he's dealing with, you can sleep off the hangover later."

"Fine, fine, no need to get surly." The blankets slid away to reveal a creased face and narrow, squinting eyes. "Werewolves: beasts of fang and claw, demons of blood and fear. The boy's doomed, end of story. Don't bother me unless one's knocking on *our* door and doesn't know the password."

"He's not doomed." Winston held up an obvious bootleg DVD, its cover an off-center photocopy. "Curse of the Werewolf. Classic Hammer." A hairy dog-faced man held an unconscious girl.

Marco rolled his eyes. "For fucks sake, the guy didn't look anything like that."

Winston fed the disc into the drive and skipped to where Oliver Reed thrashed around, still human but changing into a monster. "Look kid, from your description I'm ninety-five percent certain. The finger-eating thing is a tell-tale sign. Ghouls always go for the bone marrow and zombies the brains. No other monster eats fingers like Kit Kats."

"And the beast has your scent. It'll hunt you down," added Wu with a half-smile. "No escape. Like I said, you're doomed."

"Fucking great." Marco found a bottle of Grey Goose beside the fridge and took a pull, coughed. "I need that piece. You sell guns. That's what you do. Sell me a damn gun. Please Win, I'm begging you."

Wu half laughed, half wheezed. "You have silver bullets? Shells blessed by an honest to goodness pious priest? Is there such a thing anymore? Not that it matters, you don't look like the church going type."

"Then what the hell am I supposed to do? Leave the country?" Marco was on his feet. Screaming.

"Sit down, shit for brains, before I erase your ass myself." Winston stopped the movie. "I'd recommend you find yourself a reputable monster hunter, Nazar Safavi or maybe even Tagger Boone, but I doubt you could afford either of them."

"Unless..." Wu scratched his wispy beard. "Ever heard of Sk'elep?" He noted Marco's blank, simmering expression. "They call him the Coyote around these parts. He's old as sin, a true spirit of the earth. I felt him slinking around the shadows earlier, out for the Devil's Moon no doubt. A bit of a trickster, but if anyone can help you, he can."

"I don't know any Coyote. Who is he? A biker?"

Wu looked away. "Didn't you just listen to... no, I guess not. Look boy, you can't miss him. Bloody annoying old native fellow, probably lurking around a cemetery or a place where the dead rest, trading favours. Head over to Union or Burnsland."

Marco went white. "Fuck me," he croaked.

"Ha-ha, you've met him?"

Marco turned to Winston, eyes glazed from the vodka. "A gun. I just need a gun, any gun. I'll come back tomorrow with cash, four figures, my dad will give me a loan if I beg. Dammit Win, sell me a fucking gun already!"

The giant heaved himself out his chair and walked over to the bro, prying the bottle from the young man's hand. "You deaf, or stupid, or both? I think it's time for you to get the hell out of here. Wu wants to get back to la-la land and I got the Almost Impossible Game Show to watch." Winston dug a heavy mag light from a box of boxes and held it out. "Take this, maybe it'll even help some. I'd call you cab, but I no longer give a shit."

"Thanks for nothing." Marco snatched the flashlight and let himself be dragged back through the labyrinth.

"And I don't want to see your face around here until you learn some manners." Winston slammed the door shut.

The streets were darker now, quieter. Marco jumped with every sound, jumped with every flicker of movement. Cursing the useless Double W wankers but frustrated, lit up, and tired of running, he staggered around in a deepening haze until he found the old Indian on the same bench in Central Memorial.

Coyote grinned, eyes crinkling. "I thought you might be back. Did you bring me a smoke?"

"I hear... I hear you can do something about a fucking werewolf."

"Indeed, indeed. But, before I do, I need a smoke?" He held out a hand.

"Enough about the smokes, I don't have time for this." Marco let the mag light slide through his hand till he held it like a club. "Do something now old man, or I'm going to fuck you up."

"Are you?" Coyote shook with a laugh. "You are a bit player in a grand and noble tale, a throwaway, but you might have gone the distance, learned some respect, made something of yourself."

Marco snarled and swung, the heavy black tube passing through the fading spirit. "Shit!" He swung again, overbalancing and spinning to the ground. He scrambled to get up, get back on his feet, but the beer and vodka made his head swim and his legs weigh a thousand pounds.

Skritch, skritch.

A rough-edged form detached itself from the shadow of the cenotaph, nails scraping on the plaza concrete, and drool dripping from glittering teeth.

"Help... I'll get you a pack I promise. Just help me... I'm sorry. Please..." Marco choked and crawled away, stopping dead when the moon emerged from behind a cloud and a shaft of light speared down to pin his shadow. He felt hot breath on his neck and screamed when his arm twisted behind him. The beast of fang and claw, the demon of blood and fear, growled and tore off the first finger.

14

Another Thing

The quake wracked the apartment, toppling a ceiling high stack of garbage and sending yellowed science fiction novels spinning across the floor. One slim volume rode the wave to the foot of my recliner. 'Who Goes There?' by John W. Campbell. Damn appropriate if you ask me. While this wasn't an Antarctic research base, and the present apocalypse didn't involve aliens, the similarities were uncanny. Blowing the dust off the cover, I restacked the heap and made sure the other piles weren't in danger of collapsing. Hoarder. The last word out of my wife's mouth on her way out the door, leaving me trapped under an avalanche of antique trash.

Sirens whined by, heading into the city core. I dropped back into the chair as they faded into the distance, surprised emergency services still put in an effort. "Jeeves, show me the news." Good for a laugh if nothing else. A wall of light appeared, resolving into a long distance shot of burning office towers and collapsing government buildings. The newscaster bordered on hysterical.

"... parliament has been evacuated and army reserve units have fallen back to CFB Edmonton. Among the dead are the Deputy Premier and Minister of Public Security. Premier Karensa and the surviving MLA's have been evacuated ..."

My bone phone chirped twice. I'd set the damn thing to only take emergency calls, but select people could get through the filters. In this case Magnus, my old Sergeant, older friend, and royal pain in the ass. We still got together, like clockwork, every Friday night to guzzle beer and reminisce. It was Tuesday. Morning. He never called Tuesday morning.

"Do you know what day it is? What time it is?"

"They got Pog and the Swede in Edmonton." His voice oozed rage, the edges blurred by alcohol. "With Missy on ice, it's just the two of us left." His next words were distorted by the unmistakable tinkle of breaking glass and the bellow of a garbled hymn, the latter belted out by souls exuberant and talentless.

I'd heard those saucy verses online, dollar-store lyrics resurrected by a cult of the clueless, a cult with a shiny new Calgary chapter by the sounds of it.

Magnus spoke louder, drowning out the chorus. "It's time, Sledge, it's time."

"Be right there." I dragged myself off the chair and gazed out the window. Watched the smoke rise. "Jeeves, show me the old unit, you know the one." A sixty-year-old picture appeared, all laughing faces and glazed eyes. The squad sat in the bar, dead drunk, toasting friendship and swearing to be there when the time came.

The time.

Today.

Damn blood oaths. I sighed and stumbled into the storage room, strains of the hymn echoing in my ears. Shoving comic filled bins aside, I uncovered the trap door to the cubbyhole and pried out a battered steamer trunk full of armour, weapons, and gadgets. Amid the junk I found a serviceable pair of steel-toed boots, a bulletproof trench coat, and an electro-charged broadsword. Sadly, no guns, the wife didn't want them around the house, and regardless of our differences, I'd respected her request.

I swung the heavy sword around and loosened up. It didn't take much. Modern medicine couldn't make me young, but I wasn't over the hill yet. I snagged an injector from the bathroom and gave myself a double dose of stem cells laced with invigorators. The cartridge had enough for another month, but what the hell; I doubted I'd be back any time soon. I pressed it to my neck and used it all, energy surging through my veins like wildfire.

The ground shook again, this time causing a refuse landslide. Screw it. I hauled the steamer trunk down to the parking garage and loaded it into my old cherry red Tesla-Mercedes Z Class. The vintage hot rod had a supercharged quantum engine and hadn't been street legal for years, but I drove it around the garage, past rows of identical silver auto-pods, when nobody was around. The engine roared and I rolled out on manual, blasting through the flashing traffic lights, past smoking buildings, and around shell-shocked morning commuters. Mag's place wasn't far and fifteen minutes later I pulled onto his street, a narrow lane shaded by blighted poplar trees.

A preachy, apotheosizing mob of pirates surrounded the front of Mag's house, singing their hearts out and tossing empty rum bottles in every direction. The few that hit solid surfaces exploded, raising cheers. I didn't see any weapons besides the bottles and cheap plastic cutlasses.

Standing on the steps, a middle-aged in man in a silver helmet motioned everyone to silence. Cleared his throat.

"Chapter 2, Verse 23 of the Book of Mafalde."

The new age preacher stumbled through a short incomprehensible passage. Something about the 'evils of parmesan', its meaning lost in the lack of context. When he finished, the crowd broke out in cries of "R'amen" with the occasional "Arg" thrown in for good measure. Straightening his ruffled white shirt, the preacher knocked on the door.

"Magnus Magnusson. In the name of the Holy Trenette, exit your den of perdition, confess your sins, and become one with the holy brethren."

I heard a muffled "Fuck Off" and a message echoed in my head. "Where the hell are you? I'm dying here."

Time to rock and roll. I strolled down the street, just another ubiquitous bottle picker humming a long-forgotten theme song to a long-forgotten boxing movie. A kid wearing a Jolly Roger flag smiled when he saw my sword but changed his tune when I went Eye of the Tiger on his ass and kicked him into a thorny hedge. His frantic yelp caught the attention of the rear guard. They rushed over, more curious than suspicious, and joined the boy in the bushes. With no time for further pleasantries, I carved a wide arc through the bewildered and unprepared sycophants with my sword, knees, and elbows. Anyone that got back up received extra attention. When the remaining dozen realized I was alone, they attempted to surround me, mob style. I danced back and held them at bay, breaking a few arms in the process.

The front door of the house blew open and Magnus joined the fray, a drunken Viking with a massive grey beard. His kit consisted of army boots, a utility kilt, and a hell of a lot of tattoos. In one hand, he held an old school Louisville slugger and in the other, a stick topped with cement and barbed wire. He used the first to brain the preacher, now gaping and pawing through his orange leather tome, looking for god knows what. As the man fell in a heap, the two of us made short work of the rest, reveling in a bit of the old ultra-violence. I hated to admit it, but virtual reality couldn't hold a finger to a one-sided street fight.

Once no further opposition presented itself, Magnus flipped over the moaning preacher and nudged his ribs. "I told you I wasn't interested. Why couldn't you just take no for an answer?"

The man coughed, dribbling blood from the corner of his mouth. "But it comes ... don't resist. Heaven awaits with... with a beer volcano and... a stripper factory. Free nachos."

Mags kicked the man's helmet, a stainless-steel colander adorned with tiny cheese wedges, out into the street. "I don't believe in your mumbo-jumbo. And besides, if I was going to worship fairy tales, it would be Odin. Not your weak, pathetic TV dinner of a god."

The man gurgled and lost consciousness.

I wiped the gore, hair, and torn costume fragments from my sword. "You didn't need me for this."

"True, but I didn't want you to miss all the fun. The family that slays together, stays together."

He had me there. "We might have been a bit hasty though," I stretched and sat down on the stairs, working the kinks out of my shoulders, "his heaven has a beer volcano and a stripper factory. Best offer I've heard yet."

"As if. Now hold on a sec." He disappeared into the house and returned with a couple of bottles. "I'll show you heaven. Drink heathen."

Mead. The label looked handmade and displayed an image of Cthulhu riding an eight-legged horse. We clinked bottles and chugged, watched another quake tear the street open. I wasn't a huge fan of fermented honey mixed with weird drugs, but it hit the spot and made sweet love to the chemical soup of my blood.

Magnus stopped and snorted. Spit. "Fucking Pastafarians."

The smell of uncooked noodles and old leather sandals washed over me as long noodly appendages oozed up and out of the cracked pavement, feeling and searching. Magnus charged back into the house and returned with a pair of enormous tri-barreled pistols and long green metal case emblazoned with faded yellow lettering. He dumped the box at my feet. "All yours."

I guessed this was it, end of the road. Last ride of the magnificent two. I guzzled the rest of the Mead and cracked open the case. A bulky black rifle sat in the packing foam. "Heavy sucker," I said, picking it up.

"A portable rail gun. It slices, dices, and makes julienne fries."

"Sweet."

Magnus reached over and flicked a switch. It hummed a nice little melody that soothed my roaring nerves. "Just brace it against the railing, it has one hell of a kick." He cracked his pistols open and fed in bright red cartridges while singing "This is my last roller coaster ride."

The street caved in and a nightmare pulled itself free of the smoking pavement. It rose, floating, to tower over us, lobster-like eyestalks squinting and glaring.

Mags spun his pistols. "You ever kill a god before?"

"No."

"Well, here's your chance, just don't fuck it up."

Magnus opened up, six simultaneous shots smashing my ears and ripping the air. White phosphorous shells exploded, setting the Flying Spaghetti Monster ablaze and sending burning hamburger and overcooked starch in every direction. Before it could recover, I followed up with the railgun. The depleted uranium needles cut a massive strip across the floating monstrosity, shredding tentacles and disintegrating meatball guts. Magnus reloaded and we unleashed hell on the creature until our weapons ran low on ammunition.

"The street caved in and a nightmare pulled itself free of the smoking pavement."

We let the smoke clear to admire our handiwork. The artificial god, created by an apocalyptic singularity of misplaced intelligent design, fringe cults, and self-replicating nanites, lay in a jumbled puddle, one eyestalk still functional and staring in our direction. It looked pissed off. I didn't see beer volcanoes or stripper factories in our immediate future.

"You have another clip, or uh, ammo pack for this thing?"

"No," he said, reloading his pistols, "it fell off the back of an army truck. I was happy I could get anything before they shipped the Highlanders off to the Caribbean. Did you see what the Scientologists invoked? A two-hundred-foot-tall L. Ron Hubbard and an army of Psychlos. They're still fighting those things. Losing from what I hear."

The god began pulling itself back together.

"Now what?" I asked. "I don't think we have the firepower to keep it down."

"Well if you want to bug out, we should leave a.s.a.p. Your car looks intact."

The ground shook again, toppling trees and garbage bins.

"Any point? Anywhere to go?"

"Tijuana. We could knock over a tequila distillery and drown our sorrows until the world ends." He shrugged and pulled a silver flask from his sporran.

"Right..." I snagged it from his offering mitt and took a long pull, coughed on the rotgut. "Too bad you don't have an EMP or a pocket nuke tucked away in there."

"I thought that was your specialty, Mister Wizard. You told me you were going to cobble something together in case of emergency."

"Impossible to get parts these days, especially military grade. I built a prototype, but it needs an appropriate power source, one I can overload."

"Excuses, excuses."

The FSM floated again, the lost eye reassembling as we watched. Chewed up strands of pasta uncoiled and slithered towards us so I chopped them down using tiny, focused bursts to save ammo.

"See you on the other side," I said.

Magnus looked at me out of the corner of his eye. "Nice working with you." An old joke from when movies were funny.

Screeeeeech.

A black matte armored SUV emblazoned with network news logos roared in and drifted sideways, spitting cobalt beams of burning plasma. The driver side gull wing door flipped open and a figure in ballistic nylon jumped out, bouncing over the broken roadway to hose down the FSM with exploding flechettes. Three drones followed and whirled away, cameras recording every detail. Further plasma bursts reduced the monstrosity to a writhing blob.

The cameraman waved and flipped up his visor. "Sorry I'm late, got held up in the Capital." Pog, combat photographer to the rich and famous.

Magnus raised an eyebrow, released an earth-shattering belch, and tossed him the flask. "I heard you was dead."

"It takes more than some lame Priests of Discordia to take me down. I was filming the Premier's State of Emergency speech when their goddess showed up and cratered the Legislature. Went to take a leak and missed it by that much." He pinched thumb and finger together.

"I thought you said you got that fixed," Magnus said with a smirk.

"Still an asshole I see."

"And Sven?" I asked, smiling.

Pog winced. "By the time I got to him there wasn't much left. Bits here, bits there. You know how it is. Good thing he's a cyborg, I salvaged his brain and hotwired him to the car. He's running my rig for the time being." The car flashed its lights.

I thumped Pog on the back. "Glad you made it, the Sarge started your wake early. I don't suppose you have any weapons? We're out."

The trunk popped open. "Help yourself. In case you didn't already know, the Avatar of Chaos those fools in Edmonton conjured up is headed this way. Mag's will love her, she's blonde, she's angry, and she has tits the size of..."

On cue, a massive explosion threw fire across horizon. Magnus grunted and brandished an automatic shotgun. "We can worry about that later, what the hell are we going to do about this monster? It's a tiny sliver of the real deal, but it's imprinted and it's not going to stop until it converts us."

"We need a power supply with serious burst," I said.

Pog slapped the hood. "I have one, but it's powering the car and keeping Sven alive."

I rubbed my stubble and watched the ground boil, nanites transforming pavement into monster parts. The air smelled like rotten eggs. I looked at my hot-rod, an antique beast with its quantum engine. "I have an idea. Hold on and make ready, if this works, we'll need to rocket out of here." I sprinted to the Tesla, popped the trunk, and rummaged around for the crude device I'd fashioned from bootleg schematics culled from the Dark-net. Praying the bloody thing wasn't an A.I. plant that would blow up in my face, I wired it in, set the autopilot, and let the car roll down the street.

"Thirty seconds." A short fuse, but the pasta god was getting back in the game fast and besides, the blast radius would be tiny. We piled into the SUV.

Twenty Seconds.

Pog barked at the murky sphere occupying the driver seat. "Sven, punch it and head for Banff. We can restock power, weapons, and booze at my cabin."

The car squealed, tires biting the sidewalk, and g-forces pressing me into the seat. The street blurred by. Houses. Trees. Signs.

Ten Seconds.

I felt the blast wave caress our armored skin and the surreal quiet as the electronics fried and the car systems blinked off. We crashed and bounced off a light post, dead in the water.

Pog scrambled, flicking switches on Sven's brain box. After a moment he slumped, turned to glare at me. "He always thought he'd die in bed. Poor bastard."

"Tiny blast radius. I swear." I re-ran the calculation in my head, I'd miscalculated and now something else nagged at my mind. Rotten eggs. Shit. "Hold on."

The world exploded in fire and the street thrashed like a dying crocodile, flinging us end over end until everything went black.

❖❖❖

A slap. Another. I blinked, raging headache masking other, worse injuries.

"Finally. I thought I'd lost you."

The world came into focus. Dark yet not. Night? Smoke? Crackling fire? Magnus leaned against the side of the wrecked SUV, bloody face reflecting writhing orange patterns. He tossed me the flask.

I groaned and tried to move, felt bones grind. Took a drink. "Pog?"

"Didn't make it. Lucky bastard." He motioned to the burning cityscape. Things crawled around out there. Large things.

"Gas line?"

"Yup."

"At least we killed the god. One less problem in the world, not that it matters. This is the end." I flipped him the flask, shivering despite the heat.

He nodded. "Ever wonder why they didn't take human form?"

"Sometimes, but then I think, maybe they did. Maybe they've been replacing us all along. Maybe that's why people are helping them."

"No, people are just sheep. Stupid sheep looking for free nachos."

I couldn't argue with that. "Well, now what?"

"Why don't we just... hang out for a while, see what happens."

15

Gambling with Ghosts

Hammond House burned and no one noticed. A couple walked their dog down the sidewalk, a teenage girl jammed flyers into a dented tin mailbox across the street, and a boy piled pinecones on a tree stump next door. He grinned and waved. Once upon a time I might have waved back, nodded, or even cracked a smile, but that was before one of those thieving degenerates cleaned out my car. Bastards. With a glare, I clicked the remote alarm on my Austin Mini convertible, gave them all a one-finger salute, and slammed through the gate cleaving the white picket fence.

A flash from the second floor caught my attention, a face poking out, peering down from a tall, narrow window. Young. Pale. Eyes of blue ice.

They widened when they saw me scowling, and vanished without disturbing the burning curtains.

Subtle whining and light scratching pulled me back to the yard. "Sorry boy," I said, opening the gate again to let Rex through. The hellhound puppy rubbed his head against my leg and growled at the spectral flames, lifting his leg in an attempt to put them out. When that had no effect, he lost interest and chewed a metal sign tucked between the perennials.

Hammond House
Century Home and Heritage Site
Closed for Renovations
[Check in with the Foreman before starting Work]

As if. Rules were for regular people, not a young lady of eighteen years, equal parts heaven and hell. I made my own rules, thank you very much.

I stared at the door, watching eldritch flames curl out from weathered oak. This shouldn't be, couldn't be. I'd removed the curse three months ago, snuffing the phantasmal fire, but here it was, hot and nasty as ever. Well, time to put it out. Again. I held up my hand, feeling the warmth, drawing it in, savouring it. I closed my eyes and used myself as a conduit, redirected the fire to a place I knew, a place where nothing burned, where nothing could burn.

Whoosh.

The backlash tossed me off the front step and into a juniper bush. The boy next door clapped and laughed as I staggered up, probably thinking I'd slipped and fallen. Little rodent, he'd get his someday, I swear. Brushing dirt off my leggings and extracting a branch caught in my brown curls, I saw that the flames still flickered, suppressed but not gone. "Damn it." I curled my hands into fists, digging nails into palms. Nothing ever worked the way it should. Nothing. Why was it so hard?

At least I could get inside. I knocked to see if anyone was putting in overtime and unlocked the door with a murmured spell. Fresh paint assaulted my nose as Rex and I padded down the sanded front hall to the great room. Fire tinged sunlight poured through a massive bay window, illuminating sheet covered furniture and packing boxes. Stacks of bricks sat on plastic sheets beside a disassembled fireplace.

"Mary? Boys?" My voice echoed. "Hello?" I wandered through the private museum of a house, checking each room. Despite the face in the window, the place was empty, a tomb. My temper, already on a short fuse, started to ignite. "Quit screwing around," I shouted, "You called me, remember. I don't have all bloody day."

I barked a different spell, a crappy sounding "Orior Oriri Ortus!" and a sword appeared in my hand, golden flame crackling. I didn't need to say the words, but I needed to voice my annoyance.

The top of a semi-translucent head poked out of the fireplace mantle, a face with cold blue eyes, the face from the window. "We don't want to come out."

"Why the hell not?"

"You look angry. Bad things happen when you're angry."

"I *am* angry."

The head disappeared.

Rex padded over and scratched the bricks, carving a row of deep grooves. I shooed him away, willed the sword to disappear, and sat on an artistic yet uncomfortable chair. "Mary. Look, I'm sorry, please come talk to me."

The spirit of Mary Hammond, a spectral teenage girl in a burned dress, took shape astride the hearth. She, along with her two older brothers, had died in a fire some ninety years ago, haunting the house ever since. Mary scratched Rex behind the ears. "What are you mad about, anyway?"

"Life. Stuff. The fire. Have you lost what tiny shred of vapour passes for your brains? Do you think I'm the only one who can see it? It's like a beacon. It's a wonder some predator hasn't already found you."

The shades of two young men, one short and chubby, the other tall and gaunt, appeared on either side of Mary. The ample one coughed. "Not our fault this time, Lil."

"Fine, John, tell me what happened."

George cut his brother off. "We were watching Netflix last night, thanks for setting that up by the way, and there was the whoosh of rushing wind, an explosion of light. The flames crawled out of the fireplace bricks the workers dismantled yesterday."

Of course, the bricks, I should have realized that right away. The focal point of the original fire, one I thought eliminated when I'd cleansed this haunted estate months ago.

I walked over and hefted a brick, a phantom aura of purplish flame erupting around me, spreading across the floor and up the walls. "I'll have get my books to redo the entire ritual."

"Now?" said Mary, her face falling.

"Tomorrow. Nothing is going to bother you while I'm around."

"Grand! Let's play a game. We're bored, so very bored."

❖❖❖

Poker. They'd set up a card table in a long forgotten, and well hidden, wine cellar. We slid down a set of steep steps, pulled up chairs. George picked up the dog-eared deck and shuffled like only the dead could. Before I asked, a frosty can of hard cider appeared by my left hand. Fat John waved the phantom stogie clutched in meaty fingers and raised his glass. "Cheers."

We drank. I glanced around at the mounds of junk lining the walls. Boxes, bags, and makeshift containers overflowed with shiny bits of glass, tin cans, newspapers, and books.

John blew out a spectral smoke ring. "So, what is it going to be? Texas hold 'em? Five-card draw? Your choice, Lil."

"Five Card Draw."

"Dealer's choice of wild cards," said Mary.

"With a hundred-dollar buy-in, one dollar ante." George dropped the deck on the table and pulled out a roll of crisp bills.

"Twenty, with a quarter ante. You think I'm made of money?"

"Well, yes," said John, "your grandfather *is* the Devil. Lucifer, Beelzebub, the Grand Duke of Hell. I'd imagine he's rolling in it."

"He, yes. Me, not so much."

Junk hands, one after another. Out five dollars before I knew it, I consoled myself by chugging the cider like water, determined to get my money's worth.

I pointed to a stack of blue recycling bins. "Do I even want to know where all this stuff came from?"

"Just lying around out there."

"Uh huh." More hands and my stake dwindled, eaten away by antes and bad bluffs.

"One-eyed jacks and the suicide king are wild," said Mary, spinning the cards across the table with perfect precision.

The jack of hearts, king of diamonds, the king of spades, and some trash. Three of a kind. I raised a buck and they all called, matching my feeble bet.

"I'll take two." The ten of hearts and the ten of clubs. Hot damn! Full house. When I raised a couple more dollars, John grunted and raised again. Bastard was bluffing, I could tell. The other two called and I re-raised, going all in with the last of my stake. Everyone matched and I tossed my cards to the table. "Eat hot brimstone, losers!"

George smiled and laid down his hand. Four queens. John was next with four aces. Mary flipped over a straight flush and raked the chips in. Smug smiles. Dancing eyes. Laughter.

"You cheating bastards. You god-damned cheating bastards."

Mary stood up and gave a dainty bow. "Took you long enough. I thought you had special sight, spectral awareness and all that. So easy." She pushed her shades, expensive silver Pradas, into her hair. I used to have a pair just like them. Until they were nicked... from my car... right outside the house...

My temper, already simmering, exploded. I summoned my sword and chopped through the table, sending cards, drinks, cash, and flaming fragments of wood across the room. "Damn you all. Damn you all to the Burning Hells!" Three small pops, like bubbles bursting, and the ghosts vanished, John's cigar dropping to the floor and dissolving in a puff of red tinged smoke.

Rex heaved himself up, nails clattering on concrete, and gave me a look that said, "I can't believe you just did that."

❖❖❖

I stopped and watched my grandfather through the window of the cafe before going inside. The Devil leaned back in a carved wooden chair, legs out and crossed, wearing a black pinstripe suit and flirting with a waitress by the look of it. He noticed me watching and smiled.

"Lil!" He stood up as I entered, giving me a sweeping hug and a kiss on the forehead. "It's good to see you, darling. I ordered you a double espresso."

I gave him a peck on the cheek and sat down. "Thanks, *Nonno*."

The Devil watched me, the corners of his green eyes crinkling. "How have you been?"

I stared into my cup. "You know that curse you taught me? The one you said to never use in anger?"

He ran his hand through his coiffed black hair. "Bound to happen. I'm surprised it worked; the old ones aren't very reliable in this day and age. Tell me. All of it."

So, I did.

A chuckle. "Evil. Sounds like some old haunts cheated at cards and got what they deserved."

"I'm not evil."

"Half-evil."

"*Nonno*, please, I messed up. I can't leave them down there."

He thought for a moment. "They would have ended up in the Eighth Circle, the Hall of Serpents. Full of rogues, thieves, frauds, and such. Guarded by a dragon." He had a faraway look. "The dragon."

"Can't you just expel them? They're ghosts. In-betweeners. They don't belong there."

"It's not that easy. Protocol and such."

"Then send me down. I'll find them myself."

"Absolutely not." He gave me a stern look, the same one my mother often used.

"Why not? I can take care of myself."

"Lil. I don't doubt your strength, and I certainly don't doubt your courage, but the Eighth Circle is no place for a half-trained young lady. I can't let you risk your soul over three worthless ghosts."

I balled my hands into fists. "You don't understand. I need to fix this. Everything I touch takes a hard turn. A bad turn. Not this time."

He shook his head.

"But—"

"Lil. Darling. Trust me on this one. Just let it be." He tossed a twenty on the table, stood up, and patted my shoulder. "I'll talk to you later. Eligos wants to go for a drink and beg a boon, and duty is duty."

More determined than ever, I watched grandfather leave, realizing he hadn't mentioned my most applicable attribute. Stubbornness. I'd gotten it from him, after all.

❖❖❖

An hour later I tiptoed down a dark hallway in the Devil's old country lodge, a plan spinning through my head. The living couldn't reach the Eighth Level of Hell without passing through the first Seven, a perilous and time-consuming journey, but there were direct ways to get there and back, if you knew where to look. And I did. They just depended on the Devil's prolonged absence, raw audacity, and someone who owed me a favour.

I summoned a tiny flame, just enough to illuminate the immediate vicinity and, heart hammering, stepped into grandfather's office. As expected, a swirl of embers coalesced into a form of a young man, slight, with long blonde hair and burning eyes.

"Lilim."

"Max."

"You shouldn't be here, off limits, even to you."

"It's okay. Grandfather sent me to fetch a book, sort of a rush, spur of the moment thing. Can't keep him waiting."

"He never mentioned anything."

"Like I said, spur of the moment. Please let me pass."

His eyes narrowed, catching mine, searching for truth. He didn't find any. With a disappointed shrug, he snapped his fingers, engulfing me in a burning whirlwind, a hot, uncomfortable, virtually inescapable prison. "I can't make exceptions; the Morningstar would flay me alive. I think it's best if you wait here and explain your intrusion to him personally."

Damn, I could probably find a way to escape, but that wouldn't get me into the office. I played my trump card. "It's important Max, really important." I bit my lip and caught his dead eyes. "Remember when I saved your ass from those shades in Limbo? You owe me."

He turned away.

"Every soul you sent to oblivion with that cursed blade, every soul with a reason to hate you, hot on your heels with a score to settle, but I got you out of there."

"That hasn't even happened yet."

"Yeah, but it will," I said, staring holes into the back of his head.

"I had to kill them, had to kill every damn one of them. You can't let the past cloud the future. Lucifer, your grandfather... was very clear about that."

"No doubt, but that doesn't change the fact that you owe me."

Max nodded and let me go, vanishing into a shadow. "Yes, and now you owe me."

A frightening thought for another day.

With the clock ticking, I got down to work. The rich walnut roll top desk sat open, its interior stacked with papers. I riffled through the bottom drawer and dug out a flat wooden case containing nine polished stones resembling ornate dominos. The eighth, fashioned from fire coral and rubies, bore the device of a dragon. Score. I pocketed it, helped myself to a stack of blood coins, and tried on a ring I found tucked away in a tiny alcove above a mug of Mont Blanc pens. The red brass band, fashioned of angel feathers etched with tiny harps and trumpets, slid onto my finger like it was meant for me. I held it up, watched it shimmer in the dim light. A magic ring could come in handy where I was headed, I'm sure grandfather would agree.

❖❖❖

Two notes rested on the kitchen table when I got home, messages from my mother. "Working late," and "Wok Box in the fridge. Love you."

I mouthed a silent thank you, gorged on noodles, and pulled on a leather coat. Rex whined, tongue hanging from the side of his mouth and drool making a mess of the hardwood. "I wouldn't dream about going without you, boy. Ready?" He barked and ran around me, full of puppy exuberance as I cut my palm with a steak knife and gripped the scarlet stone tight, letting the blood do its work. With a *whoosh*, the air grew hot and we found ourselves in the depths of Hell.

Crumbling brick stairs wound down to an unmarked silver gate. No handle, no lock, just two towering slabs of gleaming adamant. I placed my hands on the silvery metal and warmth streamed into me. My pulse raced. The ancient gate, built during the First War, resisted my will. I dug deeper, summoning strength from the heavens to augment the demonic spell. It was enough. Just.

The great doors opened, sliding outwards and away, to reveal a comfortable white room dominated by a squared obsidian desk. It reminded me of the waiting room at my dentist. There were no other exits. An elfin woman with long golden hair and retro brass spectacles sat behind it, reading from a leather-bound tome.

Not bothering to look up she said, "Dropping off or picking up?" Words repeated a thousand times.

"Picking up."

"Case number and authorization?"

Bureaucrats. Hell overflowed with them. I looked at Rex. He sniffed a hanging tapestry and began circling a potted tree. Sigh. Time to improvise. Nothing beats a bit of bravado when dealing with clerks.

"Not important. I'm here to collect three souls. They should be waiting."

The woman raised an eyebrow. "Not without a case number and authorization."

Rex didn't like the tone of her voice. He growled, his eyes flaring red and smoke leaking from his nostrils.

"Fine, fine. Tell your hound to mind his manners. Names?"

"John, George, and Mary Hammond. Ghosts. They arrived earlier today."

She flipped through her book, running her finger across several pages. A tap. "Banished for cheating at cards. Why in the Hells would you want them?"

"That—" I fixed her with a frown and smoothed my jacket. "That's not your concern. Just release them into my custody and we'll be on our way."

"Hmm." The woman stood up, dropped her glasses and the book, and walked around the desk. She wore a shirt of black scales over tight leggings. Knee high boots. There was a glowing purple gem on her forehead, obscured by her hair. "Who sent you? Onoskelis? Valefar?"

I put my hands on my hips and glowered. "No one sent us."

"Then who are you?"

"Fetch the ghosts. NOW!"

"No, I think not." A sword of black fire appeared in her hand and she swept it around, intent on a quick kill. I turned the blade with my own, the golden flame leaving a bright arc. She paused to look at me, my weapon, and Rex. Recognition flashed across her face. "So, HE sent you, did he? That good for nothing rat bastard." She smiled, a terrible smile, and attacked with a flurry of lightning cuts, forcing me back.

"Well, damn you then." The curse was an explosive blast across the room.

She laughed and didn't miss a beat. "That spell won't work here. You can't damn the damned." It was all I could do to stay on the defensive, reversing step-by-step towards the gate. Rex darted around behind her, looking for an opening where he could put his teeth and claws to good use. The woman was strong. Skilled. I knew at once I was outclassed. She did too. A vicious strike smashed through my guard, leaving a deep cut in my coat and shoulder, another across my thigh. "Go home, little girl. Come back when you learn how to fight."

Damn it.

She neglected Rex for a moment. Just a second, but it was enough. He got his razor-sharp teeth around the back of her calf and bit down hard. She screamed, taking her eyes off me, and turned to deal with the ravaging hellhound, kicking him hard, flinging him across the room and over the desk. My blade, relegated to my off hand, flicked out, but the slice, meant to take her head off, merely licked her forehead.

She slid back and wiped the blood from her eyes, her beautiful face twisted with demonic fury. Red-black drops hit the tiled floor, scarring the white stone. "You'll regret that."

An aura of darkness manifested, turning her skin jet black and twisting her features until they became serpentine. She drew in a deep breath and gave me a draconic smile.

Double damn it.

I held my sword in a guard position, knowing it wouldn't help, and grasped for a spell, any spell that might help. Nothing came to mind.

She let out the pent-up air, a superheated cone of dragon fire, and the inferno washed over me, disintegrating the colourful tapestries and scorching the walls. I closed my eyes and cursed in defiance.

A dull roar, a warm summer breeze; somehow, I expected more. Pain maybe? A tingle crept up my arm from the red brass ring forgotten on my finger, a cool cocoon of angelic light.

The dragon lady poured it on, intent on turning me into a pile of ash. I pushed through the billowing fire until the point of my sword pressed against her throat. "Enough," I shouted.

The flames died away.

I held the blade as steady as I could. "I don't know anything about your issues with my grandfather and, frankly, I don't care. I'm just here for the bloody ghosts."

She gave me a hard look and clicked her tongue, still pissed off, but wavering. "Fine." The dark aura and sword faded away and a doorway appeared at the back of the room. "You'll find them out there with the rest of the gutter trash, now leave and don't come back."

Mumbling a healing spell to close my wounds, I summoned Rex and staggered out into the smouldering cityscape.

"And tell your grandfather this isn't over. Not remotely." The edge was back in her voice as the portal closed behind us.

❖❖❖

The burning neon streets teamed with all manner of demon, a supercharged Vegas blending Mardi Gras with Day of the Dead, slow instrumental jazz with thrash metal, and old beer with embalming fluid. An odd fusion, sure, but I'd expected a lot worse from the Cesspit of Hell.

While I absorbed sights, sounds, and smells, and wondered, quite literally, where in Hell the Hall might be, a glorified golf cart swung to the curve and a thin man with Elvis hair lit up a million-dollar smile. "Ma'am. Need a lift? A guide? Honest Thom is here to help."

Too good to be true, but I didn't have much choice. "I need to get to the Hall of Serpents. Know it?"

His mouth opened, black cigarette hanging from his lip, and he gave me a once over. "I might know it."

I flipped him a blood coin.

It disappeared into a pocket with a nod. "It's not far. Hop in, your hound can ride in the back."

"Thanks."

He pulled out into traffic and turned on a small fan, blasting the back seat with searing air. "No air conditioning, sorry, another day, another stupid prohibition. Not that I care about laws, mind you, but enforcement has been brutal."

"I'll live," I said, shrugging out of my dragon-ventilated jacket and flicking away a pint of sweat.

His glance bounced off the rear-view mirror. "So, you're a dancer?"

Ha! "Right."

"Thought so. Beautiful up-circle girls don't walk out of *that* door and ask for the Hall unless they're working. Or royalty. And you look like a dancer, move like one."

Well, at least one vote of confidence. I shrugged, tried to look confident, tried to remember some dance moves I'd learned years earlier. Ballet, tap, hip-hop, you name it, but I'd never put in much effort, just another time-consuming activity my mother used to keep me busy, out of trouble, out of her hair. I missed it, to tell the truth, the camaraderie with the other girls, the physicality, getting lost in the music.

Rex barked at someone or something that appeared canine. It barked back. He looked happy, tongue hanging out, wind deforming his jowls.

"The Hall is a rough place, if you didn't already know that, but they always get the best talent. You'll be a hit in that outfit," said Thom as we pulled up to a massive nightclub, its pulsing green sign displaying a writhing bucket of snakes. "I'll come by later and check out the show. Save me a seat." He winked.

"Thanks again." I dropped a few coins into his hand, hopped out, and scratched Rex between the ears. "Well, boy, here we are."

Heavy beats pounded, bass low enough to shake the sidewalk and the line of ugly riffraff circling the block. They howled at us, whistling and catcalling until a slab of doorman pushed through and interposed.

"Backstage is the fancy glowing portal to the left of the bar. Missy will get you settled in." He gave Rex an eye. "No dogs allowed."

Even heaven had fewer rules than this bloody place. "I need him. He's my... He's part of the... my routine."

The man blinked for a second, his imagination kicking into overdrive. "Uh, okay." He waved us by, muttering to himself. What little I heard made me blush.

Grog guzzling patrons lounged along endless white oak tables, heads coming up, eyes ogling, sizing me up, stripping me down. I took a deep breath and pressed forward to the bar, searching for my wayward ghosts. No dice. A band played in one corner while a semi-nude albino succubus hung from a silver pole by her tail, grinding her hips in time with the music, the circular stage below awash with coins. I was tempted to give it a go, get a picture, leave it somewhere by accident so mother would have a cow.

Rex growled as a group of large, bull headed nightmares flowed out of the gloom to surround us. Spiked hooves and beards of scarlet flame. Horns pierced with metal rings. They crowded around.

The largest leered at me. "New blood. Finally! Come give old Aym a private show." He patted sinewy thighs while his companions bellowed and snorted. One of them groped my ass.

"Keep your hands to yourself, Ferdinand," I said, straightening my shoulders and cocking my head. I'd met their type before. Cowards. Show a little spine and they'd lose interest. Besides, I was in a crowded bar, what could they possibly do?

"Ah, a spirited one. Boys, bring her downstairs."

Two minotaurs grabbed my arms and started pulling. Damn. "Let me go, meatheads." I tried to pull away, twisting to kick one in the nuts, but he just laughed and shook me hard enough to produce whiplash. A rough hand wrapped around my mouth when I invoked a curse. The bar patrons didn't even look up from their drinks.

Thank god for Rex. He snarled and pounced, shredding tattooed arms, forcing them to drop me, forcing them back, and giving me a moment to regain my bearings.

Aym urged the bulls on. "Take her, kill the hound."

Screw that noise, I summoned my sword and sheared through demon hide, spraying molten ichor that pitted the floor.

"Bitch!" Aym bellowed, spitting fire. "Kill them both." Clubs and blades replaced happy fingers. I blocked Aym's overhand swing, shearing through the haft of his two-handed axe and leaving him surprised and off balance. Before I could finish him off, another of the herd slammed into my back, smashing me to the ground, my sword spinning away to dissolve in a burst of rainbow pyrotechnics. Hooves came in hard and pain exploded through my side. Ribs shattered. I screamed, lungs heaving, the pain distorting my vision, but saw a flash of black as Rex tore into the big demon. Trying to concentrate enough to manage a quick healing spell, or one to cut the searing pain, I rolled under a vacated bench as another hoof clipped my shoulder. Just a moment, dammit, I hadn't gotten one word out before the bench flipped aside and huge, bloodshot eyes glared down at me, a mouth twisted in a smile. *Crunch*. The bull man shook and dropped like a rock.

"Sorry ma'am," said the doorman, kneeling to examine my bleeding side. "No excuse for this sort of thing in here." He tugged the leather out of the wound as I gritted my teeth. "Meridiana will fix you right up, once she's done with the brute."

Aym wasn't looking good. He hung from the air and clawed at his beard, a white rope coiling around his neck and throat, eyes bulging and mouth gaping, pleading wordlessly. With a sharp *crack*, he jerked and thrashed, dropping to the ground with a thud.

The owner of the rope, or tail as it turned out, leapt from an overhead beam and landed beside me. Meridiana. The succubus. She murmured a spell and scarlet tendrils wrapped my chest, easing the pain and knitting the broken bits back together. I wouldn't be exerting myself anytime soon, but I could take it from here.

"Thank you."

"The least I can do, darling." She purred, the same way my grandfather did, and helped me up.

Rex. In the excitement, I'd forgotten about him. I looked around, took a cautious step, and spotted him behind a pile of beef, gnawing on a broken piece of horn, happy as could be. Figures.

The succubus put her hands on her hips, thrust her chest out. Gave me a critical eye. "You aren't the new dancer, are you?"

"No. I—" She put a finger to my lips and smiled, raising my temperature a dozen degrees.

"Too bad. You have it."

Spinning with unearthly grace, she smiled and padded back to the stage, pausing for a second to whisper over her shoulder. "When you change your mind, come talk to me, I'll be waiting."

My heart pounded, and not from the fight. Grandfather had been right, this wasn't a place for a half-trained young lady. I was way out of my league, running on adrenaline and luck. Neither would last. But. Always the "but." I'd defied my grandfather, stolen his treasures, and forced my way across a deep corner of Hell. I couldn't quit. I wouldn't quit.

Wiping the sweat from my forehead and the blood from my jacket, I pushed myself between a couple of bleary-eyed ghouls and dropped a coin on the bar top. The grizzled old tender nodded once and slid over a ceramic mug ringed with tiny hammers. The drink tasted dark and stormy. Liquid courage.

I took a long pull and wheezed. "I'm looking for three ghosts. Probably showed up a few hours ago."

He rubbed his chin and thought for a moment, then tilted his head to stairs leading up to the second floor.

It didn't take long to find them, holding court at a battered table surrounded by various underworld fiends. I stopped and watched them fan the flames of avarice. They were good at it.

Mary spotted me and ran over, throwing her arms around me and squeezing until I almost blacked out. "Lil! What on earth are you doing here?"

"I got you into this mess. I thought I'd better get you out of it."

"Oh." The three of them looked at old battered me, looked at the huge pile of coins on the table in front of them, and then looked at the rest of their card-playing companions, an odious collection of infernal thieves and crooks.

I knew what she was going to say before she said it.

"You shouldn't have! We like it here. A bit warm, but our new friends are making us comfortable." Their big stupid grins were back. "Join us for a game? Texas hold 'em. Two blood coin ante. No limit."

One of the players, a weasel in more ways than one, offered up his chair.

I sat down. "Let me get this straight. You don't *want* to leave?"

"Hell no," said George.

"Never," said John.

"Why would we?" asked Mary.

I didn't know whether to laugh or cry. For the first time in a long time, I wasn't even mad, just tired and a trifle vengeful. "Fine. Then give me my stuff back. All of it."

With sheepish smiles, they pulled out items and tossed them into a pile: a handful of change, a necklace, two pairs of earrings, and sunglasses. Everything valuable I'd misplaced near their house, including the bracelet I'd worn to the afternoon's poker game.

"Really?" I felt my wrist. Sure enough, it was gone. "For Heaven's sake!"

Pop... pop... pop...

❖❖❖

The Devil sat at the kitchen table reading the newspaper and drinking tea. Without looking up, he tapped the section he was reading. "The sum of all evil can be summed up in four words. Letters to the Editor."

I groaned and collapsed into my chair, the smell of fresh toast making my mouth water. Grandfather got up, poured a tall glass of chocolate milk, and placed both toast and milk onto the mat in front of me. Grunting a hoarse "thank you," I drained the glass and started shoveling. Rex found his bowl overflowing with grim and glistening chunks of who knows what and did likewise.

"Mission accomplished?" he asked, folding the paper and tossing it into the recycling basket.

"Sort of."

His eyes twinkled.

"You never listen, do you?"

"Nope."

"So, what did you learn from your little adventure besides breaking and entering, blackmail, and theft?"

I wiped the crumbs and milk from my lips with a sleeve. "Always know your case number and authorization."

He laughed.

"Oh, and I need a loan."

"For what? You already owe me for what you took, most of which I'd like back by the way."

"Studio fees. I'm dancing again."

16

Last Call

The Devil drained the tumbler and rolled it between his fingers, admiring the delicate starbursts etched in the crystal. Waterford Wedgewood, the proper way to enjoy fine whiskey.

A light touch to his shoulder. "Another sir? Last call."

He nodded to the waitress. "Please, and one more Bloody Caesar for the lady. Make it a double."

Death looked up from her cell phone and raised a sharp eyebrow. "As tasty as they are, as you are, I'm not getting involved in your... crusade. I walk the line between light and darkness. I can't take sides."

"I'm not asking you to take sides, I'm asking you to turn a blind eye."

"A debatable distinction."

"Come now, haven't you been listening? I'm at war here."

"So? Your tales were entertaining. I'll give you that. But fishing? Really? You'll have to do better, offer more."

"I know what you want, who you want," he said, "but it's out of the question. I need Max. Do you know how many assassins they've sent so far this year?"

Tossing her phone onto the table, Death stirred her newly arrived drink with a slender piece of celery and licked salt from the rim of the glass. "Five."

"Yes, five. The boy excels at his job, I'm lucky to have him."

"I wouldn't call that luck." She smiled. "Then how about Lil? Your granddaughter intrigues me. Would she be up for an apprenticeship? I think we could help each other."

The Devil took a sip of his Lagavulin, savouring the flavour before letting it slide down his throat. "I'll tell you what, next time you buy, and you tell the stories, and I'll see what I can do."

LINER NOTES

When the editor of this book asked me to write some liner notes, which is a tradition with Coffin Hop Press books, I was a little hesitant. Who wants to read my opinion of my own stories? That same editor pointed out that every story has a story, and that I have a good one...

I know the Devil. He was there as I grew up, watching over me, teaching me, giving me spending money when I returned his stubby beer bottles or worked his farm. He was a dark soul, full of fire, full of anger, old and tired but with a twinkle in his eye if you knew when to look. You see, the Devil was *my* grandfather.

I pulled *Fishing with the Devil* from my memories of him. Memories of drinking beer as a child. Memories of blasting across mist covered lakes in search of elusive sea monsters. Memories of choices. This story was a finalist in the 2015 Robin Herrington Memorial Short Story Contest and published in *In Places Between 2015*.

Lil's adventures continue in *Gambling with Ghosts*, published as *Hot Blooded* in the *Enigma*

Front: Burnt anthology, and probably won't stop there.

The Devil, obviously, is at the heart of this collection. Not only my grandfatherly version of him, but various incarnations that pop up in different stories throughout. Why the Devil? What is it about him? Isn't he normally portrayed as a villain? Definitely. But isn't he also intriguing? I think so. He's evil incarnate, but he's also a fallen angel. He's the red-headed stepchild of Creation. He may be a bad guy, but he's just playing his part in a system he had no hand in making. Maybe he's not so bad after all. Maybe he's the good guy, and we've all been misled... Case in point: Is Santa Claus just a jolly bringer of toys and good fortune, or is he maybe a frighteningly vindictive elf with a troubling agenda and OCD? He's got that list. He's checking it and checking it. You don't want to get on the fat man's bad side. Who knows where the truth really falls? The Devil does. And he's willing to push poor little Max, drenched in blood, fire, and *Secret Hate*, to do something about it.

Speaking of red-faced pitchfork enthusiasts - I first met Axel Howerton at his quarterly event #NoirbarYYC (one of the first, and best, "Noir at the Bar" events in Canada). When he mentioned Coffin Hop Press was developing an Albertacentric crime anthology - *AB Negative* - I knew I had to submit. I wrote up this pitch for *Dead Reckoning* and sent it in:

"Tagger Boone isn't a hard man to kill. In fact, his entire life has been a slow dance with various shades of death. As a finder of people, places and things in Calgary's dark underbelly, he has a certain knack for getting the job done while taking an uncanny, and often lethal, amount of abuse. The ultimate cost of doing business."

When the beautiful and enthusiastic Lien Hua wants Tagger to find her honourable ancestor Master Wu, he knows for certain he is getting in over his head. Even with help from a hard drinking, skirt chasing, knee capping dwarf with a superiority complex, it won't be a sure thing."

They liked the story and published it, dragging me into the world of crime writing. I started writing more of the same, writing darker. Then I found myself drawn to it. I kept diving into the deepest end, the blackest part of the pool.

Noir conjures up images of doom and hopelessness, where poor choices lead to self-destruction and nobody gets out alive. I love how Otto Penzler describes it: "A Noir story will end badly, because the characters are inherently corrupt and that is the fate that inevitably awaits them." Lovely stuff.

While taking a course on Noir and Hardboiled fiction, I was challenged to come up with a sci-fi story infused with Noir style and elements. *Rust* took a ton of drafts, and was a bitch to write, but in the end, it turned into something special.

It didn't stop there, however. What's just as fun as sci-fi noir? Grimdark and a little story called *The Sharp Edge of the Moon*. What do monsters consider fast food? Vampires: blood. Ghouls: bone marrow. Zombies: brains. Werewolves? The lore is a bit fuzzier on that one, but according to Axel Howerton's delicious gothic werewolf novel, *Furr,* Lycanthropes love fingers. They can't get enough, gobbling them down like *Kit Kats* whenever the opportunity presents itself. I borrowed that fact, and a minor player from Axel's novel, when I opened a side-door from his world into mine. In addition to being a fun homage, this story introduces Winston and Wu, the seemingly idiotic owners of the Double-W pawn shop. Two bozos itching to become notorious. Luckily for them, the wheel spins round and round, and they just might show up in the future, whether it's in Axel's world, or my own.

It's no secret that I'm a massive fan of John Carpenter. The imagery. The music. The insanity. The adventures of John Nada, Snake Plissken, Jack Burton, and R.J. MacReady are forever etched into my memories, leaking out when I least expect it. One such leak became *Another Thing*, an homage I began - a hell of a long time ago - when I sat in a bar, dead drunk, doing shots with my buddy Ragnar. He put his arm around me, looked me in the eye, and said, "When it's all over, when we're spent, I'm going to call you. It's time, I'm going to say, *It's time*." I'm still waiting for that call, but it's going to come. One day.

Less homage, but no less humorous, *A Hole* is the tragic fable of what can happen when you drink too much, and get tangled up with the wrong girl. Poor guy should have just run for it.

I run, for fun, and for exercise. To challenge myself. To meditate. Sometimes I run for an hour. Sometimes twelve. I work on stories as I go, grinding ideas, working through problems. It's no surprise, that running, or the heart of what running means to me, bleeds into my stories.

Sometimes, when I'm out there on the verge of a heart attack, I think about death. Specifically, where does a runner go when they die? Heaven? Hell? I suspect the best of us end up in Purgatory, straining towards the finish line but never quite reaching it. Other times I think about running on other planets, about running on Mars. While struggling up some massive, steep mountain, I was struck with an idea about two extreme athletes running up Mons Olympus. That seed germinated a dozen times. It became a ghost story, a horror story, and even a romantic adventure. In the end? *Running the Red* is a human-versus-nature story, bursting with hard science, mortal suffering, romance, and daring rescues.

I grew up steeped in swords and sorcery: *Conan*, *Fafhrd and the Gray Mouser*, *Kane*, *Elric*. While I rarely write fantasy, I was encouraged to come up with a story, based on the Knights of the Round Table, for an anthology. I didn't want to just write a traditional piece about a run-of-the-mill knight in shining armour – I needed an off-the-wall spin, a different take with a different sort of hero, a hero with special *Strength.*

Another foray into the perilous realms became the story *Fallen.* I wanted to spin a tale where the Church was the last bastion of hope and order in a Steampunk world, a world where fallen angels gathered power to reignite the war in the heavens. Where righteous machines fought angelic clockworks. This story was a finalist in the 2016

Robin Herrington Memorial Short Story Contest and published in *In Places Between 2016*.

I've always been a huge fan of *The Gashlycrumb Tinies* by Edward Gorey: twenty-six sad, unsuspecting children meeting a veritable smorgasbord of untimely and terrible deaths. Classic and clever. I decided to do the same, only with author friends, and instead of a simple rhyme, I'd write a story, a piece of flash fiction, describing a possible fate. Thus, was born *The Deathlyflash Unfortunates*. *The Fourth Horseman*, originally entitled *Jacks are Wild*, started life as one of these stories. The titular Jack is none other than Jack Castle, adventurer, stuntman, and spinner of the fantastic.

And finally, *The Dragon's Eye*, an attempt at a Stephen King type story, full of nostalgia, childhood drama, and supernatural menace. It's easy to become the thing you hate most. Enough said.

Thanks for reading, and watch out for the Devil in Nonno's coveralls.

Robert Bose

ROBERT BOSE

MENTIONS

The devil is in the details, they always say, and writing a book is no exception. Luckily, I had help, from, well, a variety of angels. Karen, Garrett, Carter, and Alexa, who put up with my crazy schedule and late-night muttering in the dark. The Bose and Hughes Clans, sometimes overwhelming but always supportive. Sarah L. Johnson, who panned gold from a river of mud, bravely stomping adjectives and holding me a higher standard. Axel Howerton, for teaching me the writing biz and letting me elbow my way into his brilliant world. Jim Beveridge, for providing a visual glimpse into my crazy, twisted universe. My countless friends – I'm not ignoring you, I swear! And finally, special thanks to Jenn Fitzgerald, for freeing the Devil and setting me on this course.

ROBERT BOSE

ABOUT THE AUTHOR

Photo Credit: Todd Kuipers

Robert Bose grew up on a farm in southern Alberta and spent every free moment reading whatever he could get his grubby paws on. His genre-spanning fiction has been published in *nEvermore! Tales of Murder, Mayhem and the Macabre*; *AB Negative; Enigma Front: Burnt*; and *Biketopia*. Robert is currently working on a supernatural mystery novel while ultra-running, annoying his wife, raising three troublesome children, and working as the Director of Innovation for a small Calgary software company.

Find him online at **www.robertbose.com**

New Crime. New Weird. New Pulp.

Visit us online at
www.coffinhop.com

Made in the USA
Middletown, DE
29 September 2017